The Adventures of Sherlock Holmes

GLOBE BOOK COMPANY, INC.

New York/Cleveland/Toronto

The Adventures of Sherlock Holmes

Arthur Conan Doyle

adapted classic tales

Olive Eckerson
formerly of Glendale High School
Glendale, California

Wallace R. Murray
formerly of San Jose State University
San Jose, California

Illustrations by Ned Glattauer

Third Edition 1984

ISBN: 0-87065-046-7

PRINTED IN THE UNITED STATES OF AMERICA
7 8 9

About the Author

Arthur Conan Doyle was born in Scotland in 1859. He was interested in medicine and after finishing medical training set up his own practice. Among his favorite authors were Edgar Allan Poe, the first detective story writer, and Wilkie Collins. Collins was the father of the English horror story.

To please his wife, Doyle began to think about writing a detective story. He remembered the writings of Poe and Collins and set himself to follow in their footsteps. Doyle wanted his master detective to be striking in appearance. The detective would have to be very clever, absolutely fearless, and have an unusual manner. Above all, he must be a man with a special charm of his own. But Doyle felt he also needed someone to tell the stories. And he decided that it ought to be a doctor, like himself. And so Sherlock Holmes and Dr. John Watson were born.

Thus began the writing career of Arthur Conan Doyle. When his first stories appeared in the *Strand Magazine,* there were no great books on criminology (the study of crime). Doyle had to depend on his powers of deduction and observation to solve the problems he created for Holmes.

By 1890, Doyle had given up medicine to devote himself to writing. Soon he was famous. The tall, lean figure with the peaked cap and pipe, answering to the name Sherlock Holmes, was known almost everywhere. Doyle had intended to write only six stories, but the public would not let him drop Holmes and Watson. But drop Holmes he did. When people read of the supposed death of Holmes and his enemy Moriarty at the foot of Reichenbach Falls, (see page 70) they were stunned. But Doyle remained firm. Later Doyle gave in—a little. He wrote a play called *Sherlock Holmes.* The play was a huge success both in England and in America.

In 1899, England was at war in South Africa. Doyle decided to enlist. He got an appointment as an army doctor. The king wanted to reward Conan Doyle by making him a knight. At first Doyle refused. But eventually the soldier-author became Sir Arthur Conan Doyle. At the age of 43 he was the world's most popular writer. Still he refused to bring Holmes "back to life."

Finally, in the spring of 1903, he gave in. Doyle wrote "The Adventure of the Empty House" and Holmes returned to his eager fans.

In 1907, Doyle married again. To please his new wife, he wrote several more Holmes stories. When World War I broke out, Doyle again volunteered. After the war, Sir Arthur began to study spiritualism. He continued to write and went on several speaking tours. In July, 1930, Arthur Conan Doyle died. His memory will live forever in the immortal characters of Sherlock Holmes and Dr. John Watson.

Adapter's Note

In preparing this edition of THE ADVENTURES OF SHERLOCK HOLMES, the author's main purpose has been kept in mind. Since the stories were originally published, however, language has changed. We have modified or omitted some passages and some vocabulary in the stories. We have, however, kept as much of the originals as possible.

Contents

Preface

Almost everyone in the world is familiar with the famous detective Sherlock Holmes. Tall and thin, his sharp face alert, his manner quiet and mysterious, Holmes met some of the worst criminals of his time. And he beat them.

Sherlock Holmes and his friend Dr. John Watson were created by Arthur Conan Doyle almost 100 years ago. Until the appearance of Holmes, the detective story was not popular. The first real detective story was published by Edgar Allan Poe in 1841. It was called "The Murders in the Rue Morgue." The first full-length detective novel was written by Wilkie Collins. It was called *The Moonstone.* Arthur Conan Doyle used many of the features of both stories. But Doyle went on to create the most famous detective in the literary world.

Without the aid of a central fingerprint file, mug books, telephones, blood typing, computers, or ballistics experts Holmes solved many difficult problems. He depended mostly on his powers of observation and reasoning. And the record of many of his cases has been left by his friend, Dr. Watson.

Not only will you find the action, mystery, and occasional horror that Dr. Watson recorded, but you will also find some good, exciting stories.

Read how Holmes and Watson first met. Follow them as Watson records, and according to Holmes, exaggerates, these interesting cases. And enjoy their often hair-raising adventures.

A Word From Doctor Watson

My Dear Friends:

My only claim to fame is through my long and close friendship with the famous detective, Mr. Sherlock Holmes. Had it not been for him, the world would never have heard of me. I should have passed a quiet and uneventful life as a doctor, practicing my profession in Kensington, at the west end of London.

It was rather by chance that I first met Holmes. I began my career as an army doctor and went out to India, where my work and almost my life were at once cut short by a nasty wound. For some weeks I lay in a base hospital, and was well on my way to recovery. Then I was struck down by an attack of tropical fever that nearly killed me. When I could travel, I was sent home and soon was discharged from the army. Having no relatives at all, I went to live in a small hotel in London.

But my money was fast running out, and I thought I must look for cheaper lodgings. Here fate took a hand. On the very day that I decided this, I ran into Stamford, another doctor. As we chatted, I learned that a friend of his, a man called Sherlock Holmes, was then working in the chemical laboratory of the hospital. He was looking for someone to share rooms with him. He did not have much money, either, so we were both in the same fix.

And that was how it all began. A meeting was arranged, and my friend, Stamford, told me a few things about Holmes. But I was really not prepared for the unusual personality of the man who was to become my closest friend. Stamford said that Holmes was a cold-blooded scientist. When we entered the laboratory where he was working, he struck me as anything but that.

1

I saw a figure bending over a Bunsen burner who looked up as we entered and shouted, "I've got it! I've got it!" He turned and fairly ran toward us with a test tube in his hand. It seemed that he had succeeded in some small experiment with human blood. But if he had discovered a rich gold mine, he could not have been more delighted.

I eyed him curiously. He was very tall, over six feet, and so thin that he appeared to be much taller. His eyes were sharp and piercing. His thin, hawklike nose gave him the appearance of alertness and decision. His chin was square and firm. All in all, he was a most distinguished looking man.

We were introduced and shook hands. His grip showed astonishing strength, but later on I was to see those thin hands engaged in the most delicate tasks. He immediately informed me that I had lately been in Afghanistan, and at my blank look, he chuckled. Then I thought Stamford must have told him, but such was not the case. I soon learned that Holmes possessed peculiar powers of observation which enabled him to know many things about a stranger at first glance.

We took rooms at 221B Baker Street. After we moved our things, we settled down to bachelor life. I was still not very strong, and never went out in bad weather. Instead, I spent my time in studying my new friend.

I found he had a keen mind, which he used only for certain things. He was not interested in literature, history, or politics, and not very much concerned with the usual sciences. In fact his knowledge of science was strangely limited. He knew a great deal about the human body and had a deep understanding of chemistry. His knowledge of plants was confined almost entirely to a study of poisons, about which he seemed to know everything. He was fascinated by crime literature. He knew every detail of every horror that had been committed within the last hundred years. He played the violin very well, and proved to be an excellent swordsman and boxer. And this about covered the formal education of Sherlock Holmes.

His habits were curious. He was fearfully untidy. Holmes loved to work in a litter of books and papers, while sending up clouds of tobacco smoke from a strong-smelling pipe. His methods of working, however, were neat and careful. His interest in crime led him to choose odd friends. One of them was a Mr. Lestrade, a pale, rat-faced fellow, who called frequently to see him. Lestrade was an inspector of homicide with the police force of Scotland Yard.

As other strange people would call on Holmes, he very often gave me astonishing details about them which he could not possibly have known beforehand. On first meeting people, Holmes could tell their occupations, general health, what part of the country they came from, whether or not they were married, and what they had most recently done. At first I thought he was guessing, but later I knew he was drawing careful conclusions from accurate observation.

Although I began to build up my practice, and saw a few patients every day, my chief interest was in the movements of my companion. I began to keep diaries and journals of his work. When he solved the mysteries of *A Study in Scarlet* and *The Sign of Four,* I kept careful notes. I intended someday to publish a book of these adventures. More and more I neglected my work to help Holmes. Frequently I accompanied him on his strange trips in and about London. He never went armed and depended on me to use my service revolver and my skill as a shot that I learned as an army officer. Had I not fallen in love and married, I might have given up my own work entirely. This made it necessary for me to leave Holmes and settle down to my own profession.

Holmes stayed on at our old rooms in Baker Street, buried among his books and chemical instruments. He continued to assist the local police in clearing up crimes that they could not solve, and I saw very little of him. Now and then I heard that he had gone abroad, to Russia or Holland, for example. His name would often be linked with some sensational crime which he cleverly solved. He began to be famous at home and abroad, and won the respect of both the London and Paris police.

Occasionally he would call on me and persuade me to take a brief holiday with him somewhere in England or on the Continent. My wife would go to visit her relatives, and I would go off with Holmes, always on the track of some criminal, where we both would take risks that we had no right to take. I was a married man, happily living with a wife whom I dearly loved. Holmes was fast becoming the foremost champion of the law of his time. Neither of us could well be spared. Still, we continued to have adventures in which we usually were successful.

Much to Holmes's amusement, I wrote careful accounts of all of his cases. They later were published under such titles as *Adventures of Sherlock Holmes, Memoirs of Sherlock Holmes,* and *The Case Book of Sherlock Holmes.* He used to declare that for a doctor, I was most unscientific, and that I allowed my emotions to run away with me too often when writing of him.

Was Holmes ever in love? I doubt it. He was not fond of women, although his treatment of them was courteous and gentle, even when the women proved to be the blackest of criminals. I did not often hear him refer to his relations, but he did tell me a good deal about his brother Mycroft, who was seven years older than he. Holmes admired his brother immensely. He always said that Mycroft would make a much better detective than himself, were it not for the fact that his brother was so lazy that he preferred sitting in an armchair and thinking about a case rather than going out and doing something about it.

One night I met Mycroft at his club. I found him even stranger than his brother Sherlock. He was immensely fat and took snuff from a tortoise-shell box, brushing away the grains from his enormous front with a scarlet silk handker-chief. A short conversation with him and Sherlock convinced me that what the latter had said was quite true. Mycroft was the more brilliant of the two brothers. Occasionally he would bestir himself to assist Holmes in a case, but only when, by so doing, he could save his brother's life.

When my dear wife died I had no heart for medicine. I sold my small practice in Kensington, and went back to live with Holmes in Baker Street. There I lived until my second marriage, when I left Holmes for good. He continued to work on his amazing cases until early in the twentieth century, when he announced his retirement. He then went to live on his farm near Eastbourne, where he nursed his rheumatism and studied agriculture.

I cannot close this little account without some mention of Mrs. Hudson, the long-suffering landlady who looked after our rooms in Baker Street. She was a Scotch woman of strong common sense and iron nerves who grew used to the strange procession of weird characters that passed through her house.

She would be roused at any hour of the night to admit tramps, sailors, women in distress, or gentlemen with staring eyes and wild faces who demanded to see Sherlock Holmes immediately. She became quite used to seeing Holmes departing or arriving in any one of his brilliant disguises. Sometimes he would be made up as an old crippled woman, or a bearded foreigner. At other times he would be a fat priest or a withered bookseller. Mrs. Hudson was always equal to the occasion. She was a remarkable woman.

In this little book I have recorded for your entertainment a few of the most interesting and exciting of the dozens of cases that Holmes, with my humble assistance, was able to solve. There were dozens more that I never had time to write down.

I hope you enjoy reading about my friend. I begin with Holmes's own favorite, "The Adventure of the Speckled Band."

Yours sincerely,
John H. Watson, M.D.

The Adventure of the Speckled Band

I was sharing rooms with my friend Sherlock Holmes in Baker Street at the time that these horrible and extraordinary events took place. I remember it was in April, 1883, that I awoke one morning to see Holmes standing, fully dressed, by my bedside. As it was only a quarter past seven, I was surprised to see him, for he was usually a late riser.

"I'm sorry to wake you, Watson," said Holmes. "But there is a young lady who insists on seeing me. Mrs. Hudson is already up, and rather grumpy, if you ask me, at having to leave her bed at this hour."

"I thought it must be nothing less than a fire to get you up," I said.

"No, Watson, no fire. But something quite as exciting, I fancy. When young ladies wander about the city at this hour of the morning and get sleepy people up, they must have something important to tell. I thought you would not want to miss it."

I would not have missed it for anything, and lost no time in getting on my clothes and following my friend downstairs to the sitting room. There we found a young lady, heavily veiled, and dressed in black, who rose as we entered.

"Good morning, madam," said Holmes cheerfully. "My name is Sherlock Holmes, and this is my intimate friend and associate, Dr. Watson. You may speak as freely before him as before myself. I see Mrs. Hudson had had the good sense to light the fire. We shall soon have a cup of coffee for you, for I see you are shivering."

"It is not cold which makes me shiver," said the woman in a low voice.

"What, then?"

"It is fear, Mr. Holmes. It is terror." She raised her veil as she spoke, and we could see that her face was all drawn and gray, and her eyes were those of a hunted animal. Although she seemed a woman of about thirty, her graying hair made her look much older. Holmes gave her a quick glance.

"You must not fear," he said, speaking gently, and patting her arm. "We shall soon set matters right. You have come by train this morning, I see."

"Do you know me, then?"

"No, but I observe the second half of a return ticket in the palm of your left glove. You must have started early, for the drive you took in a dogcart was a long one, over muddy roads."

The lady gave a violent start and looked bewildered.

"There is no mystery, dear madam," said Holmes, smiling, "the left arm of your jacket is spattered with mud, and the marks are fresh. Only a dogcart throws up mud in this way, and then only when you sit on the left-hand side of the driver."

"You are quite right," said she.

The lady then told us that she had started from home before six o'clock, taking the first train to Waterloo Station.

"I can stand this strain no longer. I shall go mad if it continues. I have heard of you, Mr. Holmes, from Mrs. Farintosh, whose problem you solved. Oh, sir, do you not think you could help me, too?" she asked.

"I cannot pay you anything now," she said. "But in six weeks I shall be married, with the control of my own income, and then you will not find me ungrateful."

"I ask no payment whatever," said Holmes. "All I ask is that you pay any expenses that might occur while we are working on your case. And now, perhaps you will give me the details, so that I may form an opinion of the matter."

"That is just the trouble," said the lady. "I have no definite information, that is, nothing that might lead to a solution of my problem. I only know that I am terribly afraid, and when I turn to the one person who might be able to comfort me, he puts me off with soothing words, and does not believe anything I tell him. He says I am just a nervous woman. But, Mr. Holmes, it is more than that, I assure you."

"I am listening, madam."

The lady then told us a strange story of her family.

"My name," she said, "is Helen Stoner, and I am living with my stepfather, Dr. Roylott, who is the last survivor of the Roylotts, one of the oldest families in England."

"I have heard of them," nodded Holmes.

"Although at one time the family was immensely wealthy, by the end of the last century, most of the wealth had been gambled away by heirs, who lived only for pleasure. Dr. Roylott's father dragged out a horrible life there, on the family estate, and my stepfather determined that he would not spend his life in this way.

"So he borrowed money, took a medical degree, and went out to India, where he obtained a large practice, for he was a clever doctor. But in a fit of anger over some robberies that had taken place in his house, he beat his native butler to death, and only just escaped paying for this crime with his life. As it was, he spent a long time in prison, and at length, returned to England, a bitter and disappointed man.

"While he was in India, Dr. Roylott married my mother, Mrs. Stoner. My father was a young major in the Bengal Artillery, and my twin sister Julia and I were tiny babies when he died. We were only two years old when my mother remarried. Mother had quite a lot of money which she gave entirely to Dr. Roylott while we lived with him. Under the terms of an agreement, we were to be provided with a large annual sum when we married.

"Shortly after our return to England eight years ago, my mother was killed in a railway accident. It was then that Dr. Roylott gave up trying to practice medicine in London, and took us to live with him in the old family house at Stoke Moran. There was enough money for all our wants, and for a time, we were happy.

"Then a terrible change came over our stepfather. He shut himself up in the house, and refused to have anything to do with the neighbors and old friends of the family. If he did come out of seclusion, it was only to quarrel violently with anyone who crossed his path. The men of his family have all had violent tempers, and my stepfather's is the worst of all. He quarreled and fought with so many people that no one dared to speak to him.

"Last week he threw the local blacksmith over a bridge into a stream, and I was obliged to pay a large sum of money to hush up the matter. His only friends are the wandering gypsies who roam the countryside. They have permission from him to camp on the edges of the estate. Sometimes my stepfather wanders off with these gypsies and is gone for weeks.

"Another strange thing about him is his passion for Indian animals, and at this moment he has a cheetah* and a baboon,

* *cheetah:* a large cat, something like a leopard.

which wander freely about the grounds, to the terror of the village folk. You can imagine what a life my sister Julia and I led; no servant would stay with us, and for a long time, we were obliged to do all our own housework. Although my sister was not thirty at the time of her death, her hair had already begun to turn white, as mine has."

"Your sister is dead, then?"

"She died just two years ago, and it is of her death that I wish to speak to you. At Christmas two years ago, Julia went to visit an aunt of ours, and there she met a young major of marines. When she returned, she was engaged to marry him. My stepfather did not seem to object; but two weeks before her wedding day, my sister met with a terrible death."

Sherlock Holmes had been leaning back in his chair with his eyes closed, and his head sunk in a cushion, but now he opened his eyes a little and glanced across at his visitor.

"Tell me about it," he said. "Do not leave anything out."

"That will be easy, for I remember it all as if it were yesterday. It was so awful that I shall never forget it. The manor house is very old, and we live in just one wing. The bedrooms are on the ground floor, the sitting rooms being in the central block of the building. Dr. Roylott has the first bedroom, my sister had the second, and I have the third. Do I make myself plain?"

"Perfectly so."

"The windows of the three rooms open out on the lawn. On this particular night, Dr. Roylott had gone to his room early, but we knew he was still up, for we could smell the strong Indian cigars he always smoked. Julia left her room to get away from the smell, which she hated, and chatted with me about her approaching marriage until about eleven o'clock.

"Just as she was about to leave, she turned and said, 'Tell me, Helen, have you ever heard anyone whistle in the dead of the night?'

" 'Never,' I said. 'Why do you ask?'

" 'Because during the last few nights, at about three in the morning, I have been awakened by a low, clear whistle. I cannot tell where it came from, perhaps from the next room, perhaps from the lawn. I wondered if you had heard it.'

"Mr. Holmes, I myself had never heard it, but then, I sleep more heavily than Julia ever did. But I thought it might be the gypsies. My sister wished me good-night, and a moment later, I heard her lock her door."

"Indeed," said Holmes. "Was it your custom to lock yourselves in at night?"

"Yes. We were afraid of the cheetah and the baboon."

"I see. Please go on."

"I could not sleep that night. I was afraid of something I could not name. It was a wild night, with a howling wind and a heavy rain beating and splashing at the windows. Suddenly, above the noise of the storm, I heard my sister's terrified scream. I sprang from my bed and threw on a shawl. Just as I opened my door, I seemed to hear a low whistle and then a clanging sound, as if some heavy mass of metal had fallen.

"I ran down the corridor and saw that my sister's door was slowly opening. Then, by the light of the lamp in the hall, I saw my sister, her face white with terror, groping in the open doorway, swaying as if drunk.

"I ran to her and threw my arms about her, but she fell writhing to the floor in a terrible convulsion. I bent over her, and then she suddenly shrieked out in a voice I shall never forget, 'Oh, my God! It was the band! The speckled band!'

"Then she stabbed the air with her finger in the direction of our stepfather's room and tried to say something more. But she soon lost consciousness. I rushed out, calling for my stepfather, who came running up in his dressing gown. It was too late. Julia died without regaining consciousness. That, Mr. Holmes, was the end of my beloved sister."

"One moment," said Holmes. "Are you sure about this

whistle and the metallic sound? Could you swear to it?"

"I am almost sure I did hear it, although in the storm and the excitement, I may have been mistaken."

"Was your sister dressed?"

"No, she was in her nightgown. In her right hand we found the charred stump of a match and in her left a matchbox."

"That means that she struck a light when the alarm took place. That is important. And what conclusions did the coroner come to?"

"Oh, he was most careful, Mr. Holmes. He made a thorough investigation. The evidence showed that the door had been fastened on the inner side, and the windows had old-fashioned shutters with iron bars. The floors were found to be solid, and the chimney, though wide, is well barred. It is certain that my sister was alone when she met her end. There were no marks of violence on the body."

"How about poison?"

"The doctors could find no trace of poison."

"How do *you* think your sister died?"

"I think she was frightened to death, Mr. Holmes. But what it was, I cannot imagine."

"Were the gypsies there at the time?"

"Yes, there were nearly always some there."

"Ah, and what did you make of the allusion to the speckled band?"

"Sometimes, I have thought that my sister was delirious, and sometimes, I have thought that it referred to the band of gypsies. Perhaps the spotted handkerchiefs they wear might have something to do with it."

"I doubt it," said Holmes. "Please go on."

"All this took place two years ago, and I have been very lonely. A month ago, I became engaged to an old friend. We are to be married in the spring. The day before yesterday, some repairs were started in the west wing of the building, and my bedroom wall has been pierced. I have had to move into my sister's room and to sleep in the very bed in which she slept.

"Imagine my thrill of terror, when last night, as I lay awake, thinking of her terrible fate, I suddenly heard, in the silence of the night, the same low whistle that Julia had described on the night of her death. I sprang up and lit the lamp, but nothing was to be seen in the room. I was too shaken to go back to bed, and as soon as it was daylight, I dressed and left the house, coming at once to you."

"You have done wisely," said Holmes. "But have you told me all?"

"Yes, all."

"I do not think so," said Holmes. Leaning forward, he pushed aside the frill of black lace that hung over the woman's hand and said, "You are shielding your stepfather. By that, I see that he has used you cruelly." He pointed to five bruises, the marks of a finger and thumb, that showed darkly against the white skin.

She put her hand over the injured wrist. "He is a hard

man," she murmured. "I do not think he knows his own strength."

"I think we had better go down to Stoke Moran today," said Holmes. "Could we see these rooms without your stepfather's knowledge?"

"Yes, I believe so. He spoke of coming up to town today, so the house should be clear for some hours."

"Excellent. Watson, should you care to make this trip with me?"

"By all means."

Holmes then instructed Miss Stoner to go home and await our arrival by a later train. Saying good-bye to us, she dropped her thick black veil over her face and glided from the room.

We were a good deal puzzled by what we had heard, and we spent some little time in going over the evidence given us by the girl. We discussed the fact that there were gypsies on the place. We even considered whether the metallic clang described by Helen Stoner could have been the sound made by a shutter bar falling back into place. But there our theory stopped. We could not imagine what the gypsies might do, even if they were able to get into the girl's room.

Just at this point, the door was violently dashed open and a huge man stood in the opening. He was so tall that his hat actually brushed against the cross bar of the doorway, which he filled. His yellow, sun-burned face and blood-shot eyes were full of rage, for he was in a violent passion of temper.

"Which of you is Holmes?" he demanded.

"I am," said Holmes quietly. "And who, sir, are you?"

"I am Dr. Grimesby Roylott of Stoke Moran."

"Pray take a seat, Doctor," said Holmes pleasantly.

"I will do nothing of the kind. My stepdaughter has been here. I have traced her. What has she been telling you?"

"It is a little cold for this time of the year," said Holmes.

"What has she been saying to you?" screamed the old man furiously.

"The spring flowers will soon be blooming," said Holmes.

"Don't try to put me off!" shouted our visitor, taking a step forward and shaking his riding crop. "I know you, you scoundrel! You are Holmes, the Scotland Yard busybody!"

"When you go out, please close the door. There's rather a draft," smiled Holmes, breaking into a chuckle.

"I will go when I have had my say. I am here to warn you not to meddle with my affairs. I know that Miss Stoner has been here. I have traced her! I am a dangerous man to fall foul of. See here!" He stepped swiftly forward, seized the poker, and bent it into a curve between his huge brown hands.

"See that you keep yourself out of my grip," he snarled, as he hurled the twisted poker into the fireplace and strode from the room.

"Dear me," said Holmes. "I may not be so large as he, but if he had remained, I might have shown him that my own grip is not so feeble." As he spoke, he picked up the steel poker, and with a sudden effort, straightened it out again.

"And now, Watson, we shall have breakfast, and then I must take a trip to Doctors' Commons."*

Holmes remained at the courts till nearly one o'clock, when he returned with a sheet of blue paper scrawled over with notes and figures.

"I have had a very good morning," he said. "I have learned some interesting things about our friend the doctor. After studying the dead wife's will, and comparing the income of eight years ago with that of now, I find that Dr. Roylott has suffered rather heavily from a fall in prices. If he were to pay only one of his stepdaughters the money that the mother's will provided for them when they married, he would be practically bankrupt."

---

* *Doctors' Commons:* courts of law where wills and other legal documents are recorded.

"Then he had a very strong motive for wanting to prevent the girls from marrying," I said.

"Indeed, yes. I think, Watson, there is no time to lose. The old gentleman knows that we are aware of the situation. The sooner we get to Stoke Moran, the better. And Watson, kindly bring along your revolver. An Eley's No. 2 is an excellent argument with gentlemen who twist steel pokers into knots."

We made excellent train connections, and it seemed no time at all before we were driving in a trap through the lovely Surrey lanes. My companion sat in the front of the trap, his arms folded, his hat pulled down over his eyes, and his chin sunk upon his breast. He was buried in deepest thought. Suddenly, however, he started, tapped me on the shoulder, and pointed over the meadows.

"Look there!" said he.

A heavily timbered park stretched up in a gentle slope, thickening into a grove at the highest point. From amid the branches, there jutted out the gray gables and high roof of a very old mansion.

"Stoke Moran?" said he. The driver told us that it was indeed the residence of Dr. Grimesby Roylott. Holmes, in order to stop gossip among the villagers, had told the driver that we were here on some business connected with the repairs that were going on in the building.

"If you want to take a short cut," said the driver, "get over this stile, and use the footpath where that young lady over there is standing."

"The lady, I fancy," said Holmes, "is Miss Stoner. We will get out here, driver."

We got off, paid our fare, and set off in the direction the driver had shown us. We soon overtook Miss Stoner, who was eagerly awaiting us. When she learned that we had already met her stepfather, she grew white to the lips. But Holmes reassured her.

"You must lock yourself up tonight, Miss Stoner. If

your stepfather becomes violent, we shall take you away to your aunt's where you will be safe. Now, kindly take us to the rooms we are to examine."

The huge old gray stone house was partly in ruins, although the central portion was in better repair, and the right-hand portion, where the family resided, was comparatively modern, and there was blue smoke curling up from the chimneys. Holmes walked slowly up and down the poorly-trimmed lawns and examined with deep attention the windows of the rooms.

"This, I take it, is the room where you used to sleep, the center one your sister's, and this one next to the main building, Dr. Roylott's chamber?"

"Yes. But I am now sleeping in the middle room."

"I see. You said you moved into your sister's old room because there were repairs going on next to yours. The wall there does not seem to need repairing."

"No. I think it was just an excuse to move me from my own room."

"Ah! That is suggestive. Now, on the other side of the narrow wing there is the corridor you described? There are windows in it?"

"Yes. But they are too narrow for anyone to pass through them."

"You both locked your doors at night, so no one could approach from that side. Now, would you please go into your room and bar the shutters?"

Miss Stoner did so. After a careful examination through the open window, Holmes tried in every way to get the shutters open, but without success. There was no slit through which a knife blade could be passed to raise the bar. He tested the hinges which were firmly imbedded in the masonry. No one could have entered through these shuttered windows.

"Well, that settles that theory, I fancy," said Holmes. "Come, Watson, let us see what the inside looks like."

Holmes was interested for the moment, in the center

room, the one in which Miss Julia Stoner had met her fate. There was a huge gaping fireplace, and for furniture, a narrow white bed, a brown chest of drawers, and a dressing table on the left-hand side of the window. Two wicker work chairs and a small square of carpet in the middle of the floor were all that the room contained. Holmes drew up a chair and sat silent, while his eye traveled round and round and up and down, taking in every detail of the apartment.

"With what does that bell communicate?" he said, pointing to a thick bell rope that hung down beside the bed, the tassel actually lying on the pillow.

"It goes to the housekeeper's room, I believe."

"It looks newer than the rest of the things."

"Yes, it was put there only a few years ago."

"Your sister asked for it, I suppose?"

"No, we never used bells. We used to get what we wanted for ourselves."

"Hm," said Holmes. "Excuse me a moment while I examine this floor."

He threw himself down upon his face with his lens in his hand, and crawled swiftly backward and forward, examining closely the cracks between the boards. Then he did the same with the woodwork with which the chamber was paneled. He stared for a long time at the bed, and finally he took the bell rope in his hand and gave it a brisk tug.

"Why, it's a dummy!" he said. "It won't ring. It's not even connected to a wire. It seems to be attached to a little hook up there where the ventilator opening is."

"How very silly. I never noticed that before," said Helen.

"Strange, not silly," muttered Holmes, pulling at the rope. "There are several very odd things about this room. Why should a person want to open a ventilator into another room, when he might get fresh air by opening the window?"

"That ventilator was put in about the same time as the bell rope," said the girl.

"Well, well. Dummy bell ropes and ventilators that do not ventilate. Let us now carry our researches into the inner room."

Dr. Roylott's chamber was larger than that of his step-daughter, but was furnished as plainly. A camp bed, a shelf full of medical books, an armchair beside the bed, a plain wooden chair standing against the wall, a round table, and a large iron safe were the principal things in the room. Holmes examined each with the keenest interest.

"What's in here?" he asked, tapping the safe.

"My stepfather's business papers."

"Oh, then you have seen inside?"

"Only once, years ago. I remember it was full of papers."

"Might there be a cat in it, for example?"

"No. What a strange idea."

"Well, look at this." He picked up a small saucer of milk which stood on top of the safe.

"We don't keep a cat. But there is a cheetah and a baboon."

"Well, a saucer of milk will not go very far in satisfying so large an animal as a cheetah. There is one point which I must determine." He squatted down in front of the wooden chair, and examined the seat of it with the greatest interest.

"Well, that is quite settled," he said, rising and putting his lens in his pocket. "Hello! What have we here?"

His eye had fallen on a small dog leash which hung on one corner of the bed. The end of it was tied into a loop.

"What do you make of that, Watson?"

"It looks like an ordinary dog leash. But why should it be tied into a loop?"

"Ah, I wonder. Now, Miss Stoner, we have seen enough for the present, thank you." Holmes turned away, and his face was grim and dark. The three of us went outside and strolled up and down the lawn.

Suddenly Holmes began to speak. He was deadly serious as he gave instructions to Miss Stoner. He told her that she was to go to bed early, pretending to have a headache, and lock her door. Then, when she was sure her stepfather had retired, she was to undo one of her shutters, place a lamp in the window as a signal to us, and then creep softly into her old room. The room in the center would then be occupied by Holmes and myself.

"You know how my sister died, don't you, Mr. Holmes?" said the woman, laying her hand on his arm. "For pity's sake, tell me."

"I must have clearer proofs before I speak, Miss Stoner."

"At least tell me whether or not she died of fright."

"No, I do not think so. And now, Miss Stoner, we must leave you. It would not do for Dr. Roylott to return and find us here. Be brave, and follow out my instructions, and all will be well. We shall be watching nearby from the windows of our inn."

We had no difficulty in obtaining a bedroom at the Crown Inn nearby, from whose windows we could see the front of Stoke Moran and the windows of Helen's room quite plainly. All we had to do was to wait till we saw the signal, then make our way quickly and quietly to the mansion.

At dusk we saw Dr. Grimesby Roylott drive past, his huge form looming up beside that of the young boy who drove him. The boy had some trouble in undoing the iron gates. We distinctly heard the hoarse roar of the doctor's voice and saw the fury with which he shook his clenched fist at him. Then they drove on and we soon saw a light spring up in one of the sitting rooms.

We sat there in the gathering darkness. "Do you know, Watson," said Holmes, "I rather have a twinge of conscience in taking you with me tonight. There is a great amount of danger."

"Can I help?"

"I think I shall have to depend on your assistance."

"Then I shall be happy to come."

"Thank you, Watson."

I told Holmes that I could not understand his feeling that there was danger for us in returning to Stoke Moran that night. Holmes pointed out the details we had noted in the afternoon. There was the ventilator between the two rooms; there was a rope hanging from that ventilator down onto the bed; the lady who slept in that bed died horribly. I still could not make anything of all this.

"Did you observe anything peculiar about the bed?" asked Holmes.

"I can't say that I did."

"It was clamped to the floor. This was so that the bed could not be moved, but must stay in that one position in the room. It had to be beneath the ventilator and the bell rope."

"Holmes! I begin to see what you are hinting at. We are only just in time to prevent some horrible crime."

"Horrible and clever, Watson. When a doctor goes wrong, he is the greatest of criminals. Why? Because he has nerve and knowledge. This man has both. Before this night is over, Watson, we shall have horrors enough. Let us have a quiet pipe and try to turn our minds to something more cheerful."

* * *

If you are anxious to get on with the story, you can skip this next part, but if you like a puzzle, and have a turn for detecting, you may like to work for a moment or two on this problem. You now have all the evidence, and you know by now that the criminal in the case is the doctor, who has a strong motive for wanting to prevent his one remaining step-daughter's marriage. This he intends to do by killing her. Dr. Roylott has arranged for the crime to take place in the center room where Helen is sleeping. She will lie on a bed that cannot be moved, directly underneath a ventilator, from which a bell rope hangs onto her pillow.

Review the evidence in the doctor's room. The most interesting objects are the safe, the wooden chair, the saucer of milk, and last, but not least, the little dog leash, with the end tied into a loop. Take all these things into consideration, plus the fact that the doctor, a strange and eccentric person, has spent some years in India.

Now see if you can solve the crime before Sherlock Holmes gives you the solution.

* * *

It was almost eleven o'clock when we saw a single light flash up in a window of the dark house.

"Our signal!" cried Holmes, springing to his feet. "It comes from the middle window!"

After telling the landlord that we were going on a late visit to a friend, and that we might spend the night there, we left. Soon we were out on the dark road, a chill wind blowing in our faces, our eyes fixed on the twinkling yellow light in the middle window.

We made our way noiselessly through the shrubbery and approached the house. All of a sudden from out of a laurel bush a small dark form darted. It was twisted and hideous, and it threw itself upon the lawn and writhed as if in pain.

I started back, my heart in my throat. Holmes laughed silently. "The baboon," he whispered, his lips hardly moving.

I shuddered and could not resist a hasty glance over my shoulder. It seemed that at any minute I would feel the cheetah leaping onto my back.

We crouched under the middle window and slipped off our shoes. We dared not make the slightest noise. Carefully we swung ourselves up through the window that Helen had opened for us, and tiptoed into the lamplit room. Holmes moved the light out of the window onto the dressing table. We glanced around. The room was just as we had left it in the afternoon.

We did not make a sound. Holmes motioned for me to sit on the chair while he took his place on the side of the bed. Before he put out the light, he whispered faintly to me to take out my revolver and on no account to drop off to sleep. I was not likely to go to sleep, as I sat there, my nerves on edge.

Holmes had brought with him a long thin cane which he laid on the bed beside him. Beside this he placed the stump of a candle and a box of matches. Then he put out the light, and we were left in the darkness.

We sat there, within a few feet of each other, our eyes straining through the darkness, our ears alert for the slightest sound. From outside came the occasional cry of a bird, and once at our very window we heard the long-drawn catlike whine which came from the cheetah.

We heard the church clock strike midnight, then one o'clock, two, and three. Still, we sat, waiting.

Suddenly there was a slight gleam of light at the ventilator, but it vanished immediately. Then there was a strong smell of burning oil and heated metal. Someone in the next room had lit a dark lantern. I heard a soft movement, and then all was silent again, though the smell grew stronger. For half an hour we sat, with straining ears. Then came another sound, a gentle, soothing sound, like that of a small jet of steam escaping from a kettle.

The instant that we heard this, Holmes sprang from the bed and lashed furiously with his cane at the bell rope.

"You see it, Watson!" he yelled. "You see it?"

But I saw nothing. I only heard a low, clear whistle. At the same moment, Holmes struck a light, and the sudden glare blinded my weary eyes. He lit the candle and then I saw that his face was deadly pale and full of horror and loathing.

He had ceased to strike now and was gazing up at the ventilator, when suddenly we heard a most horrible hoarse yell of pain. It rose to a shriek, went higher and higher, until it must have aroused the very villagers from their beds.

"What can it mean?" I gasped.

"It means that all is over," said Holmes. "Take your pistol, and let us enter Dr. Roylott's room."

He lit the lamp and we went to the doctor's door. Holmes tapped twice, without answer, so we turned the knob and entered.

A singular sight met our eyes. On the table stood a dark lantern with the shutter half open, throwing a brilliant beam of light upon the door of the safe, which was open. Beside this table sat Dr. Grimesby Roylott, clad in a long gray dressing gown, his ankles bare, and his feet thrust into red Turkish slippers. Across his lap lay the leash we had seen earlier in the day. His chin was cocked upward and his eyes were fixed in a dreadful, rigid stare at the corner of the ceiling. Round his brow he had a peculiar yellow band with brownish speckles, which seemed to be bound tightly round his head. He was quite still.

"The band! The speckled band!" whispered Holmes.

I took a step forward, and in an instant his strange head began to move, and there reared itself from among his hair the squat, diamond-shaped head and puffed neck of a loathsome serpent.

"It is a swamp adder!" cried Holmes. "The deadliest snake in India. Roylott died within ten seconds of being bitten, caught in his own trap. Let us thrust this creature back into its own den before it does further mischief."

As he spoke, he drew the dog leash swiftly from the dead man's lap. Throwing the noose cleverly across the reptile's neck, he drew it from its horrid perch, and carrying it at arm's length, dropped it into the safe and clanged shut the iron door.

"And now, we can take Miss Stoner to a place of safety and notify the county police."

We broke the dreadful news to the terrified girl and saw her safely into the care of her aunt. The police concluded that Dr. Roylott had met his end while playing with a dangerous pet. The little I had yet to learn of the case I heard from Holmes as we traveled back to London the next day.

"You see, Watson, how easy it is to come to a wrong

conclusion. I was quite misled by the presence of the gypsies and the reference to the speckled band.

"It was not until I actually saw the room with the dummy bell rope and the unnecessary ventilator that I realized that whatever had killed poor Julia Stoner had to be something small. When I saw the bed clamped to the floor, I knew that whatever came into the room used the rope and the ventilator as a bridge to pass from one place to another. It was then that I thought of a snake."

"But the whistle?" I said.

"Ah, yes, the whistle. It was by means of the whistle that the doctor called the creature back to his own room. He had trained it, by using milk, to return to him when summoned. He would put it through the ventilator, perhaps every night for a week, leave it there for a time, then whistle it back. It might take a week, but eventually, the creature would bite the girl.

"An inspection of the chair in Dr. Roylott's room showed me that he had been in the habit of standing on it to reach the ventilator. Then when I saw the milk, the safe, the lash of whipcord, I was fairly sure of my theory. The metallic clang heard by Helen on the night of her sister's death was the hasty closing of the safe door on the snake.

"So, having worked all this out in my mind, I determined to take my place in the middle room and catch the doctor in the very act of using the snake to murder Helen. You can see now, Watson, why I hesitated to bring you here and why, when I heard the hiss, I lost no time in attacking the creature with my cane."

"And drove it back through the ventilator."

"Exactly. Mad with the pain from my blows, it turned upon the first person it saw. In this way, I am no doubt responsible for the death of Dr. Grimesby Roylott, but I cannot say that it is likely to weigh very heavily upon my conscience."

The Adventure of the Man With the Twisted Lip

I left the cab in which I had been riding, and groped my way down a steep flight of steps leading to a black gap like the mouth of a cave. It was in this den that I hoped to find Isa Whitney, who was an opium addict.

Not half an hour earlier Kate Whitney had come in a frantic state of mind to beg my help in locating her husband, who had been missing from home for two days. Knowing his weakness, she felt sure that he would be found in this vile opium den in upper Swandam Lane, a filthy place on the river front.

By the light of a flickering oil lamp above the door, I found the latch and entered a long, low room, thick and heavy with brown opium smoke, and terraced with wooden bunks, much like the forecastle of a ship. Through the gloom I could dimly catch glimpses of bodies lying in strange, fantastic poses, their shoulders bowed, their arms and legs flung out at weird angles. The black shadows were pierced here and there by glimmering little circles of red light that came from the poison burning in the bowls of the little metal pipes. Most of the smokers were silent, drugged into insensibility. Only a few muttered or talked to each other in low, monotonous voices.

At the farther end of the room was a small brazier* of burning charcoal, beside which, on a three-legged stool there sat a tall, thin old man, with his jaw resting upon his two fists, and his elbows on his knees, as he stared into the fire.

I waved aside the attendant who offered me a pipe.

"Thank you, I have not come to stay," said I. "There is a friend of mine here, Mr. Isa Whitney, and I wish to speak with him."

There was a movement and an exclamation from my right, and peering through the gloom, I saw Whitney, pale, haggard, and untidy, staring out at me.

"Good heavens! It's Watson!" said he. He was in a pitiable state of reaction, shaking, his nerves on edge. "I say, Watson, what time is it?"

"Nearly eleven."

"Of what day?"

"Of Friday, June 19th."

"Good heavens! I thought it was Wednesday. It *is* Wednesday. Why do you want to frighten a chap?" He hid his face on his arms and began to sob.

"I tell you it is Friday, man. Your wife has been waiting these two days for you. You should be ashamed of yourself!"

"So I am. Help me out of here, Watson, will you? Find out what I owe, and get me a cab, like a good fellow. I've got to get home to poor Kate."

---

brazier: small metal container with a grill for holding burning charcoal.

I took his arm and we walked down the narrow passage between the double row of sleepers, I holding my breath to keep out the vile fumes of the drug, and looking about for the manager.

As I passed the old man who sat by the brazier, I felt a sudden pluck at my coat, and a low voice whispered, "Walk past me and then look back at me."

I heard the words distinctly and looked down. They could only have come from the old man who sat stooped over, bent with age, thin and wrinkled, an opium pipe dangling down between his knees. I took two steps forward and looked back. I could hardly prevent a cry of surprise. The old man was sitting so that none could see his face but me. His form had filled out, his wrinkles gone, the dull eyes were full of fire. There, sitting by his little fire and grinning at me, was my old friend Sherlock Holmes.

He made a slight motion for me to approach him. As I came nearer, I saw his face had once more sunk into its expression of doddering age. "Don't make a noise," he whispered. "Get rid of your poor friend, and then we can have a talk."

"I have a cab outside."

"Then send him home in it. He's too limp to get into any more mischief at the moment. Wait outside. I will be with you in five minutes."

It was difficult to refuse any of Sherlock Holmes's requests, for they were always put in such a quiet, definite manner. And he always spoke with such an air of mastery, as if he were absolutely in control of the situation, whatever it happened to be. I sent poor Whitney back to his wife, and soon was joined by a bent, shuffling figure. He kept it up till we·were two streets away, when he straightened up with a hearty laugh.

"Don't look so shocked, Watson. I have not added opium smoking to my other vices. It was necessary for me to spend an unpleasant hour or two in that infamous den."

"I came looking for a friend, and I suppose you were on the track of an enemy."

"Quite right, Watson, one of my natural enemies. I am in the midst of a most remarkable case, and I hoped to find a clue in the ravings of those sots, as I so often have done before. I can tell you, I am not very popular with the fellow who runs the place. I have used it for this purpose before, and he has sworn to be revenged. Had I been recognized, my life would not have been worth a penny. There is a trap door at the back of the place, near the corner of Paul's Wharf, which could tell some strange tales of what has passed through it on moonless nights."

"You mean bodies?"

"Aye, bodies, Watson. We should be rich men if we had a thousand pounds for every poor devil who has been done to death in that den. It is the vilest murder trap on the whole riverside, and I fear that Neville St. Clair has entered it never to leave it again. But where is our carriage?"

He whistled through two fingers, and his signal was answered by someone at a distance, and followed by the rattle of wheels, as a tall dogcart dashed up through the gloom, throwing out two golden funnels of yellow light from its side lanterns.

By now, nothing would have kept me from accompanying Holmes on his new adventure, and I followed him into the carriage. Holmes elected to drive, and paid off his driver with half a crown.*

"Look for me tomorrow about eleven," he instructed. "Let go of the reins. So long, then!" He flicked the horse with his whip, and away he dashed.

"I'm glad you're coming with me, Watson," he said, and then drove in silence, his head sunk upon his breast, for several miles.

We were getting to the edge of the suburban villas, when he shook himself, lit his pipe, and began to talk.

---

*half a crown: at the time, four crowns equalled a pound.

"You have a grand gift of silence, Watson," said he. "It makes you a most valuable companion. My own thoughts are not over pleasant, for I was wondering what I should say to the dear little woman who is awaiting me."

"You forget that I know nothing. Where are we going?"

"We are going to the house of Neville St. Clair, that unfortunate gentleman who I mentioned a little while ago."

"And where is that?"

"The Cedars is near Lee in Kent, about seven miles out of town. Let me tell you of this case, and see what you make of it."

I settled myself to listen.

"Neville St. Clair took up residence in Lee five years ago, in May of 1884. He seemed to have plenty of money and lived in good style. In 1887 he married the daughter of the local brewer. They now have two children. He has no job, but has interests in several companies. St. Clair spends every day in town. He is a man of good habits and a good husband and father. He has no trouble paying his bills.

"Last Monday, Mr. St. Clair went into town earlier than usual. He told his wife that he had important things to take care of, and that he would bring his little boy some building blocks.

"Now, by the merest chance," said Holmes, "on that same morning, the wife received a telegram stating that a parcel of considerable value which she was expecting was awaiting her at the offices of the Aberdeen Shipping Company. You will recall, Watson, that this company has its offices near upper Swandam Lane, where you found me tonight. Mrs. St. Clair was vexed that the telegram came too late for her husband to pick up the parcel, and so decided to call for it herself. She did some shopping first, and then picked up her parcel, emerging in the vicinity of Swandam Lane at exactly 4:35. Do you follow me?"

"It is very clear."

"If you remember, last Monday was an exceedingly hot

day, and Mrs. St. Clair was walking slowly, looking about in hopes of seeing a cab, when she heard a cry, and was struck cold to see her husband looking down at her from a second-story window. She thought he beckoned to her, but then he seemed to be plucked back by someone behind him, and disappeared from her horrified gaze. She had only time to see that he still wore the dark coat that he had on when he left in the morning, but was not wearing either tie or collar.

"She rushed down the steps of the place, for it was none other than that same opium den, and tried to get up the stairs to where she had seen her husband. But two rough men stopped her and forced her back out of doors again. Frantic by now, she rushed down the lane, and by good fortune, encountered a number of policemen, and an inspector, who were on their way to their beat.

"These men accompanied her back, forced their way into the place, but to no avail. There was no one in the upper

rooms. On the whole of that floor there was only one crippled wretch, who made his home there. Both he and the proprietor swore that no one else had been up there that afternoon.

"Just as they were about to give up, Mrs. St. Clair pounced on something with a cry. It was a small wooden box of children's blocks, the toy he had promised to bring home. Then a thorough search was made, and soon it seemed evident that a horrible crime had been committed. In a back room of this floor was found a low window overlooking a wharf. Between the wharf and the bedroom window is a narrow strip that at low tide is dry, but at high tide is covered with at least four and a half feet of water. The bedroom window was a broad one and opened from below."

"A perfect place for a crime," I put in.

"Indeed, yes. On examination, traces of blood were to be seen on the window sill, and several scattered drops stained the wooden floor of the bedroom. But most conclusive of all were the clothes of Mr. Neville St. Clair. Boots, socks, hat, watch, all in fact, except his coat, were found thrust away behind a curtain in the front room. There were no other traces of Mr. Neville St. Clair."

"And have you formed any theory as to who might have done away with the victim?" I asked. "Perhaps the man who kept the place?"

"The proprietor, although a man of vile character, could hardly have been more than a minor actor in the drama, as he was at the foot of the steps to stop Mrs. St. Clair within a few seconds of her having seen her husband alive at the upper window. He denied all knowledge whatever, and could give no information concerning his crippled lodger, Hugh Boone, nor could he account for the missing gentleman's clothes.

"So much for him. Now for the sinister cripple who lives on the upper floor of the opium den, and who certainly was the last person to see Mr. Neville St. Clair. His hideous face is well known to all who go into London. He is a professional beggar, who keeps out of the clutches of the police by pretending to sell matches. He sits cross-legged in a small angle of Threadneedle Street, with his small stock of matches in his lap. Onto the floor beside him, there falls a steady stream of charity. People are sorry for him, and no one can pass without seeing him and shuddering at his pitiable appearance.

"He has a shock of orange hair, a pale face, marked by a horrible scar, which has drawn up the outer edge of his upper lip, a bulldog chin, and a pair of piercing dark eyes. He is clever at making jokes, and is always calling out to the people who give him money and then hurry past, trying not to show their pity and disgust. This is the man whom we know now to have been the last to see the gentleman we seek."

"But he is a cripple!" I cried. "What could he have done single-handed against a man in the prime of life?"

"He is a cripple in that he walks with a limp. In all other respects, he is strong and powerful. You, Watson, as a doctor, ought to know that weakness in one limb is often made up for by exceptional strength in another."

"Please go on."

"As you may well imagine, Mrs. St. Clair fainted, and had to be sent home, as her presence could be of no help in the investigation. Then the cripple was seized and searched, and bloodstains were found on his right shirt-sleeve. But he explained them by pointing to a cut on his ring finger, which he said accounted for the bloodstains near the window, where he had been standing not long before.

"He denied loudly any knowledge of the missing gentleman, or the presence of his clothes, and the police determined to wait for the ebbing tide, to uncover fresh clues. But when the tide did recede, they found upon the mudbank not Neville St. Clair, but only his coat. And what do you suppose they found in the pockets?"

"I cannot imagine."

"No, I didn't think you would guess. They were stuffed with copper money, 421 pennies and 270 half-pennies. The coat was too heavy to be swept away by the tide, but there is a fierce eddy between the wharf and the house, quite strong enough to suck out a body and carry it off down the river."

"But you said the clothes were all found in the room. Would the body be dressed in a coat alone?"

"Not necessarily. But let us look at the possibilities. Suppose this man Boone had thrust Neville St. Clair through the window. There is no human eye which could have seen the deed. What would he do then? He would see the need of getting rid of the telltale garments. He would seize the coat, then, but just as he was about to throw it out, he would realize that the coat might not sink. He hears the commotion below. There is not an instant to be lost. He rushes to where he keeps his secret hoard of coins, and he stuffs the pockets with handfuls of money, enough to ensure its sinking. He would have done the same with the other garments, but there was no time."

"It sounds reasonable."

"Well, we will accept this theory for the moment. Boone was arrested and taken to the station, but he was found to have no record whatever. He has led a quiet and innocent life as a professional beggar. So we now have to answer four questions. What was Neville St. Clair doing in the opium den? What happened to him? Where is he now? And what connection, if any, has Hugh Boone with his disappearance?"

"I confess, I can offer no help."

"No, never have I had a case which at first glance looked so simple, and yet, which presented such difficulties."

All this time, we had been whirling through the outskirts of the great town, until the last straggling houses had been left behind, and we rattled along with a country hedge on either side of us. Just as Holmes had finished, however, we drove through two scattered villages, where a few lights still glimmered in the windows.

* * *

I am now wondering what you make of all this, my friends. Have you formed any theory while Holmes has been telling me all this? What do you make of Hugh Boone, the crippled beggar, and do you, like Holmes, connect him with the disappearance of St. Clair? Do you think, perhaps, that Mrs. St. Clair knows more of her husband's disappearance than she has revealed to Holmes and the police? If your mind is now as busy as mine was that night we rode toward Lee, you will be collecting all the threads of this mystery and attempting to weave them together into some sort of solution.

* * *

"We are on the outskirts of Lee," said my companion. "See the light among the trees? That is The Cedars, and beside that lamp sits a woman whose anxious ears have already, I have no doubt, caught the clink of our horse's feet."

"But why are you not conducting the case from Baker Street?"

"Because there are many inquiries to be made out here. Have no fear, my friend, you will be most welcome. But I hate to meet Mrs. St. Clair with no news of her husband."

We pulled up in front of a large villa, and a stableboy ran up to our horse's head. Springing down, I followed Holmes up the winding gravel path that led to the house.

As we approached, the door flew open. In the opening stood a little blonde woman, clad in a light, dainty dress with touches of pink chiffon at her neck and wrists. Her face was alight with eagerness.

"Well?" she cried. "Well?" At sight of my companion's face, she gave a slight groan.

"No good news?"

"None."

"No bad?"

"No."

"Thank God for that. Come in, you must be weary, for you have had a long day."

As soon as Holmes presented me to Mrs. St. Clair, she warmly bade me welcome and apologized for her lack of hospitality. She touched my heart as she said, "You will, I am sure, forgive anything that may be wanting in the arrangements, when you consider the blow that has so suddenly come upon us."

I assured her that I was there to do what I could to help, and with no further talk, she took us into the dining room, where under a good light, we saw a cold supper awaiting us.

"Now, Mr. Sherlock Holmes," said the lady, when we were seated, "I should like a plain answer to a few questions."

"Certainly, madam."

"You can speak freely, for I am not hysterical, nor given to fainting. I simply wish to hear your real, real opinion."

"Upon what point?"

"In your heart of hearts, do you think that Neville is alive?" And then, as Holmes seemed embarrassed, "Frankly, now!"

"Frankly, then, madam, I do not."

"You think that he is dead?"

"I do."

"Murdered?"

"I don't say that. Perhaps."

"And on what day did he meet his death?"

"On Monday."

"Then, perhaps, Mr. Holmes, you will be good enough to explain how it is that I have received a letter from him today."

Sherlock Holmes sprang out of his chair as if he had been shot.

"What?" he roared.

"Yes, today." She stood smiling, holding up a little slip of paper in the air.

"May I see it?"

"Certainly."

He snatched it from her eagerly, and smoothing it out, held it under the table lamp, and examined it intently. I stood gazing over his shoulder. The envelope was a very coarse one and was stamped with the Gravesend postmark

and with the date of that very day, as it had been posted some time after midnight of the previous one.

"Coarse writing," murmered Holmes. "Surely this is not your husband's writing, madam?"

"No, but the enclosed paper is."

"Evidently the person who addressed the envelope had to go and inquire the address."

"How can you tell that?"

"The name, as you see, is in perfectly black ink, while the rest is of grayish color. Had the writing all been done at once, the whole thing would have been blotted at the same time, and would all appear grayish. But the man had written the name, and then there was a pause before he wrote the address, which could only mean that he was not familiar with it. This is only a trifle, but there is nothing so important as trifles. Let us see the envelope. Ha! There has been an enclosure here!"

"Yes, my husband's signet ring was enclosed."

"You are sure this is his handwriting?"

"Quite sure."

The letter, written in pencil on the flyleaf of a book, read as follows:

> Dearest do not be frightened. All will come well. There is a huge error which it may take some time to rectify. Wait in patience.
>
> Neville

"Hum! No watermark on the paper, and it has been pasted down by someone who had been chewing tobacco, if I am not much mistaken. Well, Mrs. St. Clair, the clouds lighten, though I do not think the danger is quite over."

"But he must be alive, Mr. Holmes."

"Unless this is a clever forgery to put us on the wrong scent. The ring proves nothing, for it may have been taken from him."

"No, no. This note is in his very own writing."

"Very well. It may, however, have been written on Monday and only posted today, early this morning."

"I know you think that is a long time, and that much might have happened between. But you cannot discourage me, Mr. Holmes. I know all is well. My husband and I are so very close. Why, only last Monday, Neville cut himself while up in the bedroom, and although I was in the dining room at the time, I rushed upstairs, sure that something had happened. Do you think I would not know if he were dead?"

"But if your husband is alive, and able to write letters, why should he remain away from you?"

"I cannot imagine."

"Did he say anything on Monday of an unusual nature?"

"No, nothing."

"When you saw him in Swandam Lane, was the window open?"

"Yes."

"Then he might have called to you or given a cry of surprise?"

"I think that was it. He seemed to throw up his hands before his face, and then, he seemed to be pulled back."

"He might have leaped back. Did you see anything else in the room?"

"No, but that horrible cripple confessed to having been there, and the manager was at the foot of the stairs."

"Quite so. And your husband, you say, had on his ordinary clothes?"

"Yes, but without his collar and tie. I distinctly saw his bare throat."

"Had he ever spoken of Swandam Lane, or showed signs of using opium?"

"Never, in either case. Never."

"Thank you, Mrs. St. Clair. Now, let us have a little supper, and then retire, for we may have a very busy day tomorrow."

It did not take me long to crawl between the sheets of my comfortable bed, for the night of adventure had tired me out. Sherlock Holmes, however, was a man who, when he had an unsolved problem on his mind, would go for days, even for a week, without rest. His concentration was intense, and there were times when he even forgot to eat.

I could see that he was preparing to sit up all night, if necessary, with his problem. He took off his coat and vest, put on a large blue dressing gown, and then wandered about the room, collecting pillows from his bed and cushions from the sofa and armchairs. These he arranged in the form of an Eastern divan, upon which he perched himself cross-legged,

with an ounce of shag* tobacco and a box of matches laid out beside him. In the dim light of the lamp I saw him sitting there, an old briar pipe between his lips, his eyes fixed vacantly on a corner of the ceiling, the blue smoke curling up from him, silent, motionless, with the light shining upon his strong, sharp-set features.

I dropped off to sleep.

A sudden exclamation from him awoke me, and I found the summer sunshine flooding in at the window. Holmes was still sitting there, but the heap of shag was gone, and the room was full of a dense tobacco haze.

"Awake, Watson?"

"Yes."

"Game for a morning drive?"

"Certainly."

"Then dress quickly. I want to get off at once." He chuckled softly, and his eyes twinkled, and altogether, he seemed a different man than the serious thinker of the night before.

* *shag:* a coarse variety of pipe tobacco.

As I dressed, I glanced at my watch. It was only twenty minutes past four, and no one was stirring. Holmes roused the stableboy who hitched the horse, while my friend was pulling on his boots.

"I want to test a little theory of mine," he said. "I think Watson, that you are now standing in the presence of one of the most absolute fools in Europe. I deserve to be kicked from here to Charing Cross.* But I think I have the key of the affair now."

"And where is it?" I asked, smiling.

"In the bathroom," he answered. "Oh, yes, I am not joking. I have just been there, taken it out, and put it in this bag. Come on, my boy, and we will see whether our key will fit the lock."

We went out to where a sleepy-eyed stableboy stood at our horse's head, and we soon were galloping past the rows of lifeless villas. Only a few vegetable carts, on their way to the city, kept us company. Those we soon left far behind.

"Although this case has been a singular one, I confess I have been as blind as a mole, Watson. But it is better to learn wisdom late than not at all."

We kept on at a fast clip until we were within the City. We crossed the river at the Waterloo Bridge Road, and dashing up Wellington Street, wheeled sharply to the right and found ourselves at Bow Street Police Station. Sherlock Holmes was well known to the force, and the two constables at the door saluted him. One of them held the horse's head while the other led us in.

"Who is on duty?" asked Holmes.

"Inspector Bradstreet, sir."

"Ah, Bradstreet, how are you?" A tall stout official had come down the flagstone passage, in a peaked cap and a braided jacket. "I wish to have a quiet word with you, Bradstreet."

---

*Charing Cross: a street corner in London, near to Scotland Yard.

"Certainly, Mr. Holmes, step into my room here."

We entered the inspector's office and sat down.

"What can I do for you, Mr. Holmes?"

"I called about that beggar, Boone, the one who was concerned with the disappearance of Mr. Neville St. Clair of Lee."

"Yes, we have him here in the cells."

"Is he quiet?"

"Oh, he gives no trouble. But he is a dirty scoundrel."

"Dirty?"

"Yes, it is all we can do to make him wash his hands, and his face is as black as a coal miner's. Well, when once his case is settled, he will have a regular prison bath. He certainly needs it, as you would agree if you saw him."

"I should like to see him, very much."

"Then, sir, come this way." He led us down a passage, opened a barred door, passed down a winding stair, and brought us to a whitewashed corridor with a line of doors on each side.

He shot open a panel in the third door on the right, and glanced through.

"He is asleep," he said. "You can see him very well."

We both put our eyes to the grating. The prisoner lay with his face toward us, in a very deep sleep, breathing slowly and heavily. He was a middle-sized man, poorly dressed, with a colored shirt protruding through the rip in his tattered coat. He was extremely dirty, but the grime on his face could not conceal its repulsive ugliness. A broad scar ran right across from eye to chin. As it healed, it had drawn up one side of the upper lip, so that three teeth showed in a constant snarl. A shock of very bright red hair grew low over his eyes and forehead.

"He's no beauty, is he?" said the inspector.

"He certainly needs a wash," said Holmes. "I had an idea that he might, and so brought the tools with me." As he spoke, Holmes opened his bag and took out a large bath sponge.

"Ha! Ha! You certainly are a funny one, Mr. Holmes," chuckled the inspector.

"Now, if you will kindly open that door very quietly, we shall soon make him look more respectable."

The inspector slipped his key into the lock, and we all entered the cell very quietly. The sleeper half turned, then settled back into a deep slumber. Holmes stooped to a water jug, moistened his sponge, and then rubbed it firmly over the prisoner's face.

"Let me introduce you," he shouted, "to Mr. Neville St. Clair of Lee, in the county of Kent!"

Never in my life have I seen such a sight. The man's face peeled off under the sponge like the bark from a tree. Gone was the coarse brown tint! Gone, too, was the horrid scar and the twisted lip. A twitch brought away the tangled red hair, and there, sitting on the bed, was a pale, sad-faced, refined-looking man with black hair and smooth skin, rubbing his eyes and staring sleepily about him. Then, suddenly, he broke into a scream, and threw himself face down on the pillow.

"Great heavens!" cried the inspector. "It is the missing man, all right. I know him from his photograph."

The prisoner turned with a reckless air. "And now that you have discovered me, what am I charged with?" he said.

"I hardly know," said the inspector, scratching his head, cap in hand. "I've been twenty-seven years on the force, but this takes the cake."

"I have committed no crime, and therefore, you cannot hold me," said St. Clair.

"No crime, but a great error has been committed," said Holmes. "You would have done better to have trusted your wife."

"It was not my wife. It was my children," groaned the prisoner. I would not have them ashamed of their father. What can I do?"

Sherlock Holmes sat down beside him and patted his shoulder. "We can keep it quiet, I believe, if you will make a clean breast of the whole thing. If you convince the police that there is no possible case against you, I see no reason why any of it should get into the papers."

"God bless you!" cried the prisoner passionately. "I would have done anything, even faced execution, to keep this blot from my family."

Neville St. Clair then told us his strange story.

He told us that he was the son of a schoolmaster in

Chester, where he was well educated. In his youth he traveled, took to the stage for a while, and finally became a reporter on a London paper. One day he was assigned to do an article on the London beggars, and it was from this point that his adventures started.

He decided to go among the beggars disguised as one of them. This was easy, as he was clever with make-up and was able to conceal his identity beneath the horrible appearance that has been described. He took up a position in the business part of the City, as a match-seller, and kept his eyes open to learn all he could of the profession of begging.

At the end of the day, to his great surprise, he found he had taken over twenty-six shillings,* a tidy sum for doing nothing but sit and look miserable.

He wrote his article for his editor, and thought nothing more of the matter. But some time later, he helped a friend out of some financial trouble, and found himself in immediate need of twenty-five pounds. He obtained a holiday of a few days from the paper, donned his disguise, and in ten days he had the money he needed.

He now began to fall out of love with his newspaper job. Why should he slave away for two pounds a week when by smearing his face with a little paint, sitting on a sidewalk, and doing absolutely nothing, he could earn as much in a single day? He had a long fight between his pride and the money, but in the end, the money won. He became a professional beggar, sitting day after day at his post, going home each night with his pockets crammed with money.

Only one man knew his secret. It was the keeper of the opium den in upper Swandam Lane where St. Clair lodged, and from which he emerged each morning in his horrible disguise. To this place he returned each evening, where he changed into the clothes of a well-to-do man about town and went off for an evening's pleasure. He paid the fellow

---

* *shilling:* at the time, twenty shillings equalled a pound.

a good sum for the use of the rooms and for keeping his mouth shut.

He soon began to grow rich. He explained to us that not every beggar in the London streets could do this, but he had exceptional gifts which made him especially successful. Not only was he very clever with his make-up, but he was blessed with a quick wit, and kept the passers-by entertained with his amusing remarks. He became a character in the City, and people were quick to single him out for special generosity. It was a poor day when he did not take in two pounds.

Then Mr. Neville St. Clair grew ambitious, took a house in the country, married, had children, and not a soul except the keeper of the opium den knew that he was really a low beggar. His wife knew he had business in the City, but she was never curious as to how he made his money.

This life might have gone on indefinitely, had not Mrs. St. Clair accidentally surprised him at his window as he was preparing to change to go home, and been attracted by his cry of amazement.

"Then," said Holmes, "the blood on the window sill came from the cut described to us by your wife, and which must have reopened and bled when you frantically tried to get rid of your telltale clothes."

"That is right, Mr. Holmes. I had not time to get rid of all of them. I had only enough time to get back into my make-up and rags, when my wife came in with the police. My disguise was so perfect that not even she recognized me."

He paused, staring at the floor of his cell. "I do not know that there is anything else for me to explain. I sent my wife the ring and the note to ease her worry by letting her know there was nothing to fear."

"That note only reached her yesterday."

"Good Heavens! What a week she must have spent!"

"The keeper of the den must have found it difficult to post a letter unobserved, as the police were watching him very closely. He probably got some sailor customer of his to post it, and the fellow forgot it for several days."

"Yes. I am sorry for that," said St. Clair.

"But tell me," said Holmes, "were you never arrested for begging?"

"Many times. But what was a fine to me?"

"Well," said the inspector, "there must be no more of Hugh Boone, if we are to hush the matter up, Mr. St. Clair. You will have to make your living some other way."

"Yes," shuddered St. Clair. "It has been a lesson to me. I have sworn to give it up."

"In that case, you may regard yourself as safe. But if you take to begging again, the whole business must come out. We cannot protect you then. And thanks to you, Mr. Holmes, for helping to clear this matter up. I wish I knew how you reach results," said Bradstreet.

"I reached this one," replied Holmes, "by sitting upon five pillows and consuming an ounce of shag. Come, Watson, if we leave at once for Baker Street, we shall just be in time for breakfast."

The Adventure
of the Blue Carbuncle

It was the second morning after Christmas, and the weather was cold and frosty. I set out to call on my friend Sherlock Holmes, to extend to him the greetings of the season. I found him lounging upon his sofa, in a purple dressing gown, smoking his pipe, and just finishing the morning papers. Beside the sofa was a wooden chair, on which hung a very seedy and battered looking hat, much the worse for wear, and cracked in several places. A lens and a pair of forceps lying near suggested that Holmes had been examining the hat.

"Are you busy?" I said. "I don't want to interrupt you."

"Not at all. I am glad to have an old friend with whom I can discuss—that." He jerked his thumb in the direction of the old derby. "There are some interesting things about that old hat."

As I warmed my frostbitten hands at his crackling fire, I said, "I suppose this thing that looks so harmless has some deadly crime linked with it that you are now investigating?"

"No, no crime," said Holmes, laughing. "Just one of those odd little incidents that will occur in a crowded city of four million inhabitants. You know Peterson, the commissioner?"

"Yes."

"It is to him that this little trophy belongs. Oh, don't look surprised, it's not his hat. I merely mean that he found it. Its owner is unknown. Now, please regard this not as a battered article of wear, but as an intellectual problem. This hat arrived upon Christmas morning, in company with a good fat goose, which at this moment is roasting in front of Peterson's fire. These are the facts:

"At about four o'clock on Christmas morning, Peterson was returning home from some holiday party, when he saw in the gaslight on Tottenham Court Road a tallish man walking toward him. The man walked with a slight stagger, and carried a white goose slung over his shoulder. As he approached the corner of the street, some toughs rushed him, and knocked off his hat.

"Raising his stick to protect himself, he swung too wide and smashed the shop window behind him. Peterson rushed forward to protect the man from his attackers. But the man, shocked at having broken a window, and seeing a man of the law advancing toward him, dropped his goose and took to his heels. The toughs had fled also, and Peterson was left in possession of the field, plus a battered hat and a Christmas goose."

"Did he return them to their owner?"

"My dear fellow, how could he? It is true there was a card attached to the bird's leg on which was written, 'For Mrs. Henry Baker,' and there are also the initials *H.B.* in the lining of the hat. But to find a Henry Baker in this city is like looking for a needle in a haystack."

"What, then, did Peterson do?"

"He brought the articles to me, knowing that even a small problem interests me. We kept the goose as long as we could until even in frosty weather it would not stay good any longer. Peterson took it home and I am left with the hat, which I have been examining, and from which I have learned some very interesting facts. You know my methods. Take the hat in your own hands, and see what you can make out as to its owner."

I took the tattered object in my hands and looked as I thought, carefully at it. It was a very ordinary black derby hat of the usual round shape, and much the worse for wear. The discolored lining had been of red silk. No maker's name, but the initials *H.B.* were scrawled on one side. Its brim had been pierced for a long, black silk elastic to be attached to the wearer's coat button, to save the hat from being lost in a high wind. But the elastic was missing, and I noticed that several of the worst places on the hat had been covered with ink.

"I can see nothing," I said, handing the hat back to Holmes.

"On the contrary, Watson, you see everything, but you fail to gather what it means."

"Then, what does it mean?"

"This hat tells me that its owner is a highly intellectual person, who was fairly well-to-do three years ago. He has now fallen upon bad times. He used to be cautious, but now he no longer cares what happens. With the decline of his fortunes, he has probably taken to drink, and this may account for the plain fact that his wife no longer loves him."

"My dear Holmes!"

"But, all self-respect has not vanished. He leads a quiet life, taking little exercise, goes out rarely, is middle-aged, has grizzled gray hair, which the barber has cut within the last few days, and he uses lime-cream on his scalp. It also is very likely that there is no gas laid in his house."

"You are certainly joking, Holmes."

"Not in the least. Do you mean to say that you have

examined this hat and you cannot tell me how I came by this information?"

"I have no doubt I am very stupid, but I must confess I am unable to follow you. How did you discover, for instance, that the man was intellectual?"

For answer, Holmes clapped the hat on his own head. It came down to the bridge of his nose.

"That should settle it," he said. "A man with so large a head must have a correspondingly large brain."

"Well, then, how did you learn that he had lost his money?"

"This hat is three years old. I can tell by the style, which was fashionable at that time. Such a hat cost a good sum. Look at the lining and the band of ribbed silk. If this man could afford to buy this hat three years ago, and has bought none since, he must have come down in the world."

"Quite true. Now, then, how about the caution and the lack of it now?"

Sherlock Holmes laughed. "Here is the caution," he said, putting his forefinger on the disk and loop of the elastic. "These are never sold upon hats. If the man ordered one, he must have been at that time a careful man, with a certain amount of foresight, since he went out of his way to take this precaution against the wind. But we see he has broken the elastic and has not troubled to replace it. This shows he no longer cares what happens to his hat. On the other hand, his self-respect has not quite fled, for he has painted the stains on the hat with ink, to try to hide the signs of wear."

"Your reasoning is sound."

"By closely examining the lower part of the lining, it is not hard to learn that the hair is grizzled, it has recently been cut, for there are some sharp clippings, and they are somewhat greasy with lime-cream. The hat is dusty with the fluffy brown dust of the house, which shows that he does not often go out, and the stains of moisture inside indicate that he perspires freely, and is, therefore, not in very good condition."

"I agree with all this. But how can you know that his wife has ceased to love him?"

"The hat has not been brushed for weeks. When I see a man with such a miserable hat on his head, I feel sure that if he has a wife, she has no care for his appearance and probably has no care for him."

"But he might not be married."

"That is hardly likely. He was bringing home the goose as a Christmas offering, with his wife's name attached to the bird's leg."

"You have an answer for everything. But how about the business of having no gas laid in the house?"

"One tallow stain, or even two, might be on a hat by chance. But when I see no less than five, I imagine the owner has been in the habit of carrying his hat upstairs in the same hand as his guttering* candle, which has dropped grease quite freely upon it. Now, are you satisfied?"

"You are extremely clever, Holmes. But, as no crime has been committed, save the loss of a goose, it all seems rather a waste of energy."

As I said this, the door flew open, and Peterson, the commissioner, rushed into the room, his face flushed and his whole expression that of a man dazed with astonishment.

"The goose, Mr. Holmes! The goose, sir!" he gasped.

"Eh? What about it? Has it come to life and flapped off through the kitchen window?" Holmes twisted about to see the man's excited face.

"See here, sir! See what my wife found in its crop**!" He held out his hand and there on the palm was a brilliantly glittering blue stone, rather smaller than a bean in size, but of such purity and radiance that it twinkled like an electric pin point in the hollow of his hand.

---

*guttering: flowing in streams. In this case, the wax would melt very fast in a cheap tallow candle.

**crop: a bird's gullet.

Sherlock Holmes sat up with a whistle. "By Jove, Peterson!" said he. "This is a treasure, eh? I suppose you know what it is?"

"A diamond, sir? A precious stone? It cuts into glass as if it were putty."

"It's more than a precious stone. It's the famous Blue Carbuncle!"

"Not the Countess of Morcar's missing gem!" I exclaimed.

"Exactly, Watson. I ought to know its size and shape, since it has been advertised in *The Times* every day lately. The reward of one thousand pounds is not one twentieth of its market price."

"A thousand pounds! Great Lord of mercy!" cried the commissioner, plumping down into a chair and staring at us.

"Ah, yes, and I have reason to know that the countess would part with half her fortune to recover that stone."

"Wasn't it lost at the Hotel Cosmopolitan?" I asked.

"Precisely so. On December 22nd, just five days ago, John Horner was accused of having stolen it from the lady's jewel case. The evidence is so strong against him that he is being held without bail, and his trial is to be held soon."

I reviewed what I knew of the case, which had been in all the papers lately. It seemed that John Horner, 26, a plumber, had been taken upstairs to the Countess of Morcar's apartments in the Hotel Cosmopolitan to solder a bar of the fireplace grate. He was shown up to the room by James Ryder, an attendant on the upper floors of the hotel. Ryder had stayed with Horner, but then he had been called away, and on his return, he said he found the jewel case forced open, the stone missing, and the plumber gone.

He immediately gave the alarm, and Horner was arrested that evening. The stone, however, could not be found. Catherine Cusack, maid to the countess, supported Ryder's evidence in all particulars. Horner struggled frantically, and protested his innocence. But it was soon learned that he had formerly been convicted and served a term for robbery, and the magistrate ordered him held for a later trial. On hearing this, the prisoner fainted, and was carried out of court.

So much I remembered plainly.

"Hum," said Holmes thoughtfully. He had been reading the account to himself, and now he tossed the paper aside.

"We now have to solve the sequence of events that connect the disappearance of the Blue Carbuncle with its sudden reappearance in the crop of a Christmas goose. The first thing to do, I fancy, is to find Mr. Henry Baker, and learn, if we can, what part he has played in this little mystery. So we shall try the simplest method first. We shall advertise."

It was obvious that if Mr. Henry Baker were anywhere in the vicinity, he would keep an eye on the papers, since the loss of a hat and a goose was too much for a poor man to sustain. Holmes quickly penciled a notice on a slip of paper advising Mr. Henry Baker that he could learn the whereabouts of his property by calling at 6:30 that evening at 221B Baker Street.

"Just take this to the papers, will you, Peterson?" he said.

"Very well, sir. And the stone?"

"Ah, yes, I shall keep the stone. And, I say, Peterson, on your way back here, just buy a goose, will you, for we must have one to give to the gentleman when he calls."

When the commissioner had gone Holmes took up the stone and held it against the light.

"What a bonny thing," he said. "Think what crimes are committed for such playthings as this. Great jewels are the devil's pet bait. This stone is not yet twenty years old, but already it has a bloody history. Two murders, an acid-throwing, a suicide, and several robberies, all for the sake of this forty-grain bit of crystallized charcoal. It was found on the banks of the Amoy River in southern China, and is remarkable in having every characteristic of the carbuncle, except that it is blue in shade instead of ruby red. I'll lock it up in my strong box, and send a line to the countess to say we have it."

"Do you think that this man Horner is innocent?"

"I cannot tell."

"Well, then, do you imagine that this other one, Henry Baker, had anything to do with it?"

"It is more than likely that Henry Baker is absolutely

innocent, and had no idea of the value of the bird he was carrying. But that we shall soon know, that is, if we have an answer to our advertisement."

Since there was nothing we could do till then, I continued my professional round of calls, and returned to Baker Street at a little after half-past six. As I approached 221B, I saw a tall man in a Scotch tam and a greatcoat buttoned up to his chin, waiting outside the door. We were shown up to Holmes's room together.

The stranger was Mr. Henry Baker.

Holmes came immediately to the point. "Is that your hat, Mr. Baker?"

"Yes, sir, that is undoubtedly my hat."

Although the stranger spoke in the cultured voice of an educated man, it was plain to see that he had come upon bad times, for his overcoat was rusty and there was no sign of cuff or shirt inside his sleeves. His voice was jerky, and he seemed to choose his words with care. He related to us what Mr. Peterson, the commissioner, had already told us of the attack on him on Christmas Eve.

"We have retained these things for some days," said Holmes, "for we felt sure that whoever had lost them would advertise. I cannot understand why you did not, sir."

The visitor gave an embarrassed laugh. "Shillings are scarce with me these days, Mr. Holmes, and as I was sure the gang of toughs who attacked me had stolen both hat and goose, I did not see the sense of wasting money advertising for them."

"Very naturally. By the way, we were forced to eat the goose."

"To eat it!" The visitor was greatly astonished.

"Yes, it would not have kept longer. But I hope this other goose here will answer your purpose equally well. It is about the size and quality of the other one."

"Certainly, certainly," said Mr. Baker, with a sigh of relief.

"Of course," said Holmes, shooting a sharp glance at me,

"we have the legs, feathers, and crop of your bird still, if you wish them."

The man burst into a hearty laugh. "Well, I think not. With your permission, I will accept this excellent bird as substitute."

"There is your hat, then, and your goose. By the way, would it bore you to tell me where you got the other bird? I am somewhat of a fowl expert myself, and I have never seen a better grown goose."

"Certainly, sir. I belong to a club and we had all put in a few pennies a week, so that at Christmas time, each of us might receive a goose. The club meets at the Alpha Inn, and it was the landlord's idea that we use this plan to make sure of our Christmas dinners. Well, if that is all, I shall take my leave. Many thanks for the return of my hat," he said. "A Scotch tam is hardly fitting for one of my age."

He bowed formally to us, tucked the package under his arm, and strode off on his way.

"So much for Mr. Henry Baker," said Holmes. "It is obvious he knows nothing about the matter. Are you hungry, Watson?"

"Not particularly."

"Then let's skip dinner, and follow this clue while the trail is hot."

A few moments later, wrapped in our heavy coats and with wooden scarfs wound about our throats, we emerged into the bitter night. We made for the Alpha Inn, a small public house in Bloomsbury, a district down toward the east end of London. We found it at the corner of one of the streets. Holmes pushed open the door of the private bar, and ordered two glasses of beer from the ruddy-faced landlord.

"Your beer should be excellent if it is as good as your geese," he remarked.

"My geese!" The man seemed surprised.

"Yes. I was speaking only half an hour ago to Mr. Henry Baker, who was a member of your goose club."

But the landlord told us that the goose had not been

raised by him. It had been obtained with two dozen others for his gentlemen from Covent Garden, from a salesman called Breckinridge.

We finished our beer, wished the landlord good night, and hurried out.

"Now for Mr. Breckinridge." muttered Holmes, buttoning up his coat. "Remember, Watson, that although we have only an ordinary goose at one end of the line, at the other end we have a man who will certainly get seven years in the penitentiary unless we can establish his innocence. It is possible that our inquiry may but confirm his guilt. In any case, we have a line of investigation which has been missed by the police. Let us follow it out to the bitter end. Faces to the south, then, and quick march."

We left Bloomsbury, and made our way down through the slums to Covent Garden Market. One of the largest stalls bore the name of Breckinridge, and the proprietor, a horsey-looking man with a sharp face and trim side whiskers, was helping a boy to put up the shutters.

It did not take Holmes two minutes to open the subject that had brought us on this bitter cold night to the drafty and almost deserted market. Breckinridge remembered selling two dozen geese to the landlord of the Alpha, but when Holmes asked him where he got the birds, he flew into a rage.

"Now then, mister," he said, glaring at us, his hands on his hips, "what are you driving at? Let's have it straight, now!"

"I only want to know who sold you the geese that you supplied to the Alpha. There's nothing to get so warm about."

"Oh, there isn't? Well, I shan't tell you, so that's what."

"Very well," said Holmes, shrugging his shoulders, "it's not important. But I still don't see why you should get hot under the collar."

"Hot under the collar, is it? Well, you'd be hot if you were as pestered as I am. I've answered a hundred questions

about them geese. One would think they were the only geese in the world, to hear the fuss that's made of them."

"Well, I have no connection with any of those people who have been making inquiries," said Holmes carelessly. "If you won't tell us, the bet is off, that's all. But I'm always ready to back my opinion on a matter of fowls, and I have a fiver* on it that the bird I ate is country bred."

"Well then, you've lost your fiver, for it's town bred," snapped the dealer.

"You'll never make me believe that."

"Will you bet, then?"

"It's merely taking your money, for I know I'm right. But I'll bet a pound, just to teach you a lesson."

---

*fiver: a five-pound note.

The dealer chuckled grimly and sent for the books. He showed Holmes that the bird was truly town bred. It had been bought from a Mrs. Oakshott, who lived at 117 Brixton Road in the City, and who supplied eggs and poultry to the market.

Holmes looked deeply disgusted and threw the money he had bet down on the counter. Without a word he turned away, I after him.

A few yards off he stopped under a lamppost and laughed in the hearty noiseless fashion which was peculiar with him.

"When you see a man with whiskers of that cut and the Racing Sheet sticking out of his pocket, Watson, you can always get him to talk by means of making a bet. I do not think I should have found out more if I had put down one hundred pounds in front of him. Well, we are nearing the end of our search. Shall we go on to this Mrs. Oakshott's tonight, or shall we wait till tomorrow? It is clear there are others who are interested—"

A loud hubbub cut short his remarks. Turning round, we saw a little rat-faced fellow standing in the circle of yellow light under the swinging lamp. He was yelling at Breckinridge who stood in the doorway of his stall, shaking his fists at the figure before him.

"I've had enough of you and your goose!" he shouted. "Bring Mrs. Oakshott here, and I'll answer her. But if you come around to pester me any more, I'll set the dog on you! What has this to do with me? Did I buy the goose from you?"

"No, but one of them was mine, all the same," whined the little man, shrinking back from the salesman's fists.

"Well, then, go to Mrs. Oakshott."

"I did and she sent me to you."

"Now, I've had enough of this. Be off with you!" He rushed fiercely forward, and the little man screeched and ran into the darkness.

"Come on, Watson," whispered Holmes. "This may save us a visit to Brixton Road."

He strode along rapidly, and soon caught up with the little man. He touched him on the shoulder, and the fellow jumped and turned a dirty white face on us.

"Who are you? What do you want?" he asked in a shaking voice.

"My name is Sherlock Holmes, and it is my business to know what other people don't know. And don't tell me this is none of my business. I know all about Mrs. Oakshott, the Alpha, and Mr. Henry Baker."

"Oh, sir, you are the very man I have longed to meet." The little man put a quivering hand on Holmes's arm. "You are the one person to whom I can talk."

Holmes hailed a four-wheeler which was passing and suggested we go to his rooms where we could be more comfortable.

"Your name, sir?" he asked politely, as the cab drew up.

The man hesitated for a moment. "My name is John Robinson," he said, glancing sideways at us.

"No, no, your real name," said Holmes. "It is always awkward doing business with an alias."

The man flushed. "Well, then, my real name is—James Ryder."

"Ah, yes. Head attendant at the Hotel Cosmopolitan, is it not? Come, step into the cab, and let us be off."

We were silent during the half-hour drive to Baker Street, and the little man sat nervously clasping and unclasping his hands. The cold had increased, and we were glad to get to the bright fire in Holmes's sitting room.

"Here we are!" said Holmes cheerily. "You look cold, Mr. Ryder. Pray take that chair there, and excuse me while I put on my slippers. Now, then! You want to know what became of those geese?"

"Yes, sir—but—"

"Ah, yes, one goose in particular. The white one with a black bar across its tail, is it not?"

"Oh, yes, sir." Ryder quivered with emotion. "That's the one, all right. Can you tell me where it went to?"

"It came here."

"Here?"

"Yes, and a most remarkable bird it proved. After it was dead, it laid an egg, the bonniest, brightest little blue egg that ever was seen. One moment, if you please."

Our visitor staggered to his feet and clutched the mantelpiece with his right hand. Holmes unlocked his strongbox and held up the Blue Carbuncle, which shone out like a star, with a cold, brilliant, many-pointed radiance. Ryder stood glaring at it with a drawn face.

"The game's up, Ryder," said Holmes quietly. "Hold up, man, pull yourself together, or you'll find yourself in the fire. Watson, help him back to his chair. He's not the criminal type, hasn't blood enough for it. Give him a dash of brandy."

Although he had staggered at the sight of the gem, and would have fallen had I not helped him, when he was seated and had drunk the brandy, he began to look better.

"I have almost all the links in my hands, and all the proof I need. There is little which you need tell me. Still, that little may as well be cleared up. You had heard, Ryder, of the blue stone of the Countess of Morcar?"

The man drew a long, shaking breath.

"It was Catherine Cusack who first told me about the carbuncle," he said in a low voice.

"I see. Her Ladyship's waiting maid. Well, you are not the first man to yield to the strong temptation to acquire sudden wealth, but you went too far with your villainy. You knew that this man Horner had been mixed up in a robbery before, and you thought he was just the one on whom to pin the suspicion. You didn't care what happened to a man who, this time, was innocent."

Ryder wrung his hands and stared, whitefaced, at Holmes, who went on.

"And so you laid your infamous plans. You made it seem that a small job in the countess's room had to be done and you managed that Horner should be sent for. The rest was easy. When he had left, you stole the jewel and raised the alarm. The unfortunate man was quickly arrested."

Ryder threw himself down on the rug and clutched at Holmes's knees. "For God's sake, have mercy!" he shrieked. "Think of my father and mother! It would break their hearts. I never did anything like this before! I never will again! I swear it!"

"Get back in your chair!" said Holmes sternly. "It is very well to cringe and crawl now, but you thought little enough of poor Horner charged with a crime of which he knows nothing."

"I will leave, Mr. Holmes. Then the charge against him will break down."

"Hum! We will talk about that. And now let us hear a true account of the next act. How did the stone get into the goose? And how did the goose get into the open market? Tell us the truth."

Ryder passed his tongue over his dry lips. "When Horner had been arrested, I wanted to get away at once, for I thought the police might search me. I went to my sister's house. Every man I met on the way seemed to be a policeman. Even though it was a cold night, sweat was pouring down my face before I came to her house. My sister asked me what was the matter, but I told her I had been upset by the jewel robbery at the hotel. Then I went into the yard and smoked a pipe, and wondered what would be best to do.

"I had a friend who used to tell me about the ways of thieves and how they could get rid of what they stole. I decided to go to him, but then I realized I might be seized and searched, and I would have the stone in my pocket. I was leaning against the wall, and looking at the geese which were waddling about at my feet. Suddenly an idea came into my head which showed me how I could beat the best detective that ever lived.

"My sister had promised me the pick of the geese for a Christmas present. I would take my goose right then, and in it would be the stone. There was a little shed in the yard, and behind this I drove one of the birds—a fine big one, white with a barred tail. I caught it, and prying open its bill, I thrust the stone down. The bird gave a gulp, and I felt the stone pass into its crop. The bird struggled, and my sister came out to see what was the matter. As I turned to speak to her, my goose broke loose and fluttered off among the others.

"I reminded her of her promise and said I was feeling which bird was fattest, and liked that one.

"'Oh, that's not the one we've set aside for you, Jem,' she said. 'Yours is that big white one over yonder. We've fattened it especially for you, and it's a good three pounds heavier than that other one.'

"'Never mind. I'll have the other, and I'll take it now,' said I.

"'Oh, very well. Kill it and take it with you.'

"Well, I did what she said, Mr. Holmes, and I carried the bird all the way to Kilburn where my friend lives.

"I told my pal what I had done, Mr. Holmes, and he laughed till he choked, and thought it was a rare joke. We got a knife and opened the goose. Mr. Holmes, my heart turned to water, for there was no sign of the stone, and I knew that some terrible mistake had occurred. I left the bird, rushed back to my sister's and hurried into the back yard. To my horror, there was not a bird to be seen."

"I presume they had all gone to the dealer's," said Holmes.

"But you had the bird with the barred tail. You put the stone in its crop. Where was it?" said I.

"Well, sir, my sister said she had two birds with that marking and she never could tell them apart. I had killed the wrong bird."

"Then what did you do?" asked Holmes.

"I rushed off as fast as I could to this man Breckinridge. But he had sold the lot at once, and not one word would he tell me as to where they had gone. I went back again and again, but as you heard him yourselves tonight, he never would give me an answer. My sister thinks I am going mad. And now—and now I am branded a thief, and I have never touched the wealth for which I ruined myself. God help me!" He broke into sobs and buried his face in his hands.

There was a long silence, broken by his heavy breathing and the measured tapping of Sherlock Holmes's finger tips on the edge of the table. Then my friend rose and threw open the door.

"Get out!" he said.

"What, sir? Oh, Heaven bless you!"

"Get out!"

He needed no more. He rushed out of the room and clattered down the stairs. The front door banged, and we heard the crisp rattle of running footsteps down the street.

"After all, Watson," said Holmes, reaching for his pipe, "I am not hired by the police to clear up their mistakes. If Horner were in danger, it would be another thing. But the case will collapse for want of evidence and the return of the stolen property. Perhaps I am committing a felony, but perhaps, too, I am saving a soul. This fellow will not go wrong again. He is too terribly frightened. Send him to jail now, and you make him a jailbird for life." He paused and smiled gently at me.

"Besides, this is Christmas, the time of forgiveness. Please ring the bell, Watson."

The Adventure of the Final Problem

It is with a heavy heart that I take up my pen to write these words, the last in which I shall ever record the curious adventures of Mr. Sherlock Holmes. It has been two years since the events that I am about to relate took place. It was not my intention ever to tell the facts regarding the final appearance of Holmes, for they are very painful for me to recall.

But my hand has been forced. Colonel James Moriarty has recently attempted, through the publication of some letters, to defend the memory of his infamous brother, the professor who perished in the same accident as that which took the life of Sherlock Holmes. The press carried only the most scanty accounts of the tragedy, and it was not until these false reports of Colonel Moriarty appeared that I felt it my duty to tell the world what really happened. For I alone knew the truth.

During the winter of 1890 and the spring of 1891 Holmes had been working abroad, engaged upon a mission of great importance for the French government. I had seen nothing of him for some months. So I was surprised to see him come walking into my consulting room on the evening of April 24th. It struck me that he was looking even paler and thinner than usual.

He read my thoughts at once. "Yes, I have been using myself up rather too freely," he replied to my unspoken question. "I have been a little pressed of late. Do you mind my closing your shutters?"

The only light in the room came from the lamp upon the table, and Holmes edged his way round the wall, and flinging the shutters together, he bolted them securely.

"There! That ought to make us safe from—"

"From what?" I interrupted.

"From air guns. No, my dear Watson, I am not crazy. I think it very sensible to guard against danger when it is close about you." He lit a cigarette and went on. "Pardon me for calling so late, and pardon me if I do not leave by the usual way but scramble over the back wall."

"What on earth for?" I asked.

He held out his hand, and by the light of the lamp, I saw that the knuckles were scraped and bleeding.

"My danger is quite solid enough for breaking hands, you see. Do you think you could get away for a week with me?"

"Well, I could, I suppose. But where?"

"Oh, France, Germany, anywhere. It's all the same to me."

There was something about the pale, worn face of Holmes that told me his nerves were at their highest tension. He sensed what I was thinking, and putting his fingertips together and his elbows on his knees, he explained the situation.

"Have you ever heard of Professor Moriarty?" he asked.

"Never."

"Now, that's the wonder of the thing! The man's influence is felt throughout London, and no one has ever heard of him. That's what makes him wonderful. I tell you, Watson, if I could beat that man, if I could free society of him, I should feel that my own career had reached its summit, and I should be prepared to turn to some quieter line in life. I have earned enough, through my services to the royal family of Scandinavia and to the French republic, to allow me to live in comfort for the rest of my days. But I could not rest quiet in my chair, Watson, if I thought that such a man as Professor Moriarty were walking the streets of London unchallenged."

"What has he done, then?"

"At the age of twenty-one, he showed promise of becoming one of the world's geniuses in mathematics. He was offered a position in one of our leading universities, and in all ways he seemed destined for a brilliant career. But a criminal strain in his blood gained the upper hand, and what promised to be a life of usefulness became an infamous and sinister career of wickedness. He was compelled to leave the university and eventually settled down in London where he became an army coach. This much is known to the world. The rest of what I shall tell you I myself have discovered.

"As you know, Watson, I have become well acquainted with the higher criminal world of London. As I have worked on my various cases, I have long been aware of some strange power, some force behind many of these crimes. For years I have tried to break through the veil and at last I succeeded in following this strange power to its source. My investigations led me to ex-Professor Moriarty of mathematical power.

"He is the Napoleon of crime, Watson. He is a genius, with a brain of the first order. He sits motionless, like a great spider in the center of his web, while he directs and organizes his many projects through dozens of clever agents. If there is a house to be robbed, a paper to be stolen, a man to be murdered, word is passed on to the professor, who organizes the matter and has it carried out."

"But suppose the agent is caught?" I asked.

"If he is caught, money is found for his defense or his release. But the central power is never caught. When at last I learned all this, Watson, I also found that the professor is fenced about with safeguards so clever that it would be impossible to get evidence to convict him in a court of law. But I have worked tirelessly for three months. At times my horror at his crimes has been lost in my admiration for his skill. Then, at last, he made a mistake." Holmes paused.

"And then?" I prompted.

"Then, Watson, I had my chance. I have woven my net about Moriarty until, in three days—that is to say on Monday next—matters will be ripe, and the professor, with all the principle members of his gang, will be in the hands of the police. Then there will be the greatest criminal trial of the century, the clearing up of over forty mysteries, and the rope for all of these villains. The only thing now is to move with extreme caution. One slip, and the whole thing might be destroyed."

"I presume that Professor Moriarty knows you are on his trail?" I said.

"Ah, yes, but he is a wily bird. Time and time again he has escaped. Never have I been so hard pressed by an opponent. However, the last steps have been taken, and only three days are wanting to complete the business. This morning, as I was sitting in my rooms, thinking the matter over, the door opened and Professor Moriarty stood before me."

"What did you do?"

"My nerves are fairly good, Watson, but I must confess I started when I saw the man who has been so much in my thoughts, standing there on my threshold. He is extremely tall and thin, his forehead comes out in a white curve, and his two eyes are deeply sunken in his head. He is pale and looks like a professor. His shoulders are rounded from much study, and his face protrudes forward, and the most horrible thing about him is a constant movement from side to side, which reminds one somehow of a reptile. He looked at me curiously.

"'Your forehead is not so big as I expected,' he said. 'And, I might add, it is a dangerous habit to finger loaded firearms in the pocket of one's dressing gown.'

"I knew I was in great danger, Watson, for in order to escape, he had to silence me. In an instant I had slipped my revolver from the drawer into my pocket, and was covering him through the cloth. He smiled and blinked and looked at me with his snake's eyes. Then he told me that I had gotten in his way once too often, and he gave me the choice of dropping my investigations or of being destroyed.

"'You must stand clear, Mr. Holmes, or be trodden under foot,' he said.

"'I am afraid, Professor,' I replied, rising, 'that in the pleasure of this conversation, I am neglecting important business.'

"He looked at me in silence, shaking his head sadly.

"'Well, well,' he said at last, 'it seems a pity, but I have done what I could. I know every move of your game. It has been a duel between you and me, Mr. Holmes, and I tell you I will never be brought to trial. You hope to beat me. I tell you that you will never beat me. If you are clever enough to destroy me, rest assured, I shall do the same to you.'

"'If I were assured that I could destroy you, I would, in the interests of the public, be persuaded to allow you to destroy me,' I replied.

"'I can promise you the one, but not the other,' he snarled, and so he turned his rounded back on me, and went peering and blinking out of the room.

"I must confess, Watson, that the interview shook me up. The man has a soft way of talking that makes what he says sound quite sincere. He means every word he says. It is from his agents that the blow will fall, so it is of no use to take police precautions against the man himself. I have, in fact, already been attacked."

"You don't say, Holmes!"

"My dear Watson, Professor Moriarty is not a man to let

the grass grow under his feet. About midday I was crossing the street when a two-horse van came whizzing round the corner. In a flash it was on me, and I only just saved myself by jumping for the sidewalk. I thought it was coincidence, but a few moments later, as I walked down Vere Street, a brick came down from the roof of one of the houses and narrowly missed my head. That was no accident. I called the police, who examined the place, but of course they found no one. After that, I took a cab and spent the rest of the day in my brother's rooms."

"Then how did you get the broken knuckles?"

"It happened on the way over here. A tough with a club tried to jump me, but I knocked him down, and the police have him in custody. Of course they will never trace any connection between the fellow on whose front teeth I have skinned my knuckles and the mathematical gentleman who is probably ten miles away somewhere, at this moment working out problems on a blackboard."

I had never admired my friend more than now, as he sat quietly checking off the day's hair-raising events.

"Will you spend the night here?" I asked, as I put some plaster on his knuckles.

"No, my friend, you might find me a dangerous guest. I have my plans all laid, and in a few days the final arrest will be made. The police do not need me to make an arrest, though my presence is necessary for a conviction. In the meantime, I think I should do well to get away somewhere, to leave the police quite free to act. That is why I have asked you to come with me. It will be a pleasure to have your company."

Holmes had laid elaborate plans for our getting out of England as quietly as possible. Before he left me, he gave me detailed instructions as to what to do. Accordingly, before I retired that night, I sent my simple luggage, unaddressed, by a trusted messenger to Victoria Station. Rising early the next morning, I set off to meet Holmes.

I first sent my man out for a hansom,* telling him not to take either the first or the second one that was offered but to take the third. This one drew up at my door, and as I entered, I handed the driver the address on a slip of paper, first cautioning him not to throw it away. We dashed to the Strand end of Lowether Arcade, and keeping the fare ready in my hand, I rushed out the moment we arrived. I raced through the Arcade, timing myself to reach the other end at exactly nine-fifteen. There, as Holmes had told me the night before, I found a small closed carriage awaiting me, and I knew it was mine by the driver, who wore, as Holmes had said he would, a heavy black cloak, tipped at the collar with red. I stepped in and was whirled away to Victoria Station in time to catch the Continental Express.

Holmes had told me to meet him at the station and to take the second first-class carriage from the front, which had been reserved for us.

Everything had gone off perfectly. My luggage was safe on the platform, and I easily found the carriage that Holmes had described. There, sure enough, was the "Reserved" sign card in the window. My only trouble was the fact that Holmes had not shown up and was nowhere to be seen. We were due to start in seven minutes by the station clock. Where was Holmes?

In vain I searched among the groups of travelers for the tall graceful figure of my friend. I spent some minutes helping an old Italian priest who had trouble making the porter understand that his luggage was to be booked through to Paris. Still Holmes had not appeared. I returned to my carriage, hoping that he might yet arrive.

Despite the reserved card sign, the old priest had entered and was making himself comfortable. I tried to make him understand that he was intruding, but my Italian was more limited than his English, and so I occupied myself with staring

---

*hansom: a small closed carriage with the driver perched on the top.

out anxiously for my friend. A chill of fear had come over me, and I began to feel sure that something had befallen him during the night. The doors to all the carriages were shut and the whistle had blown, when—

"My dear Watson," said a voice, "you have not even bothered to say good-morning."

I whirled round. The old priest had his face toward me. For an instant the wrinkles were smoothed away, the nose drew away from the chin, the lower lip ceased to protrude, the dull eyes lighted up, the drooping figure straightened. Then the whole frame collapsed and Holmes had gone again.

"Good heavens!" I cried. "How you startled me!"

"Careful," he whispered. "I have reason to think them hot on our trail. Ah, there is Moriarty himself."

The train had already begun to move, and glancing back, I saw a tall man pushing his way furiously through the crowd, waving his hand as if he desired to have the train stopped. But it was too late. We had got away.

Holmes laughed and threw off his black cassock* which he packed with his priest's hat in a handbag.

"Have you seen the morning paper, Watson?"

"No."

"You haven't seen about Baker Street then?"

"Baker Street?"

"They set fire to our rooms last night, but there was no great harm done."

I gasped. This was past everything.

"Evidently they thought that I went home yesterday, and they certainly have taken the precaution of watching you, Watson, as we know by Moriarty's presence here this morning. Could you have made a slip in coming?"

"No, indeed. Everything went off perfectly. I am confident I left no trail for them to pick up."

"Did you recognize the coachman in the black cloak?"

"No."

"It was my brother Mycroft. It is an advantage to have a relative that you can trust; so much better than a paid servant. But we must plan what we are to do about Moriarty now."

"Well," I said, "this is an express and the boat connects with it, so I should think we have shaken him off very well."

"My dear Watson, you evidently did not understand me when I said that this man was quite as intelligent as myself. Do you think, if I were the pursuer, I should allow myself to be thrown off so easily?"

"What do you think he will do?"

"He will do what I should do. He will engage a special,

*cassock: a black robe worn by a Catholic priest.

and since our train stops at Canterbury, and there is a fifteen minute delay at the boat, I should think he will catch us easily."

"Let us have him arrested there."

"And ruin the work of three months? No, my dear Watson, on Monday we shall have them all, both the big fish and all the little ones. We cannot risk an arrest now."

"What then?"

"We shall get out at Canterbury, make a cross-country journey to Newhaven, and so over to France. Moriarty will again do what I should do. He will get on to Paris, watch for our luggage, and wait for us to show up at the depot to claim it. In the meantime, we shall buy a couple of carpetbags and make our way, by a roundabout route, to Switzerland."

At Canterbury, we found that we had an hour to wait before the train for Newhaven came in. I was still staring after my disappearing luggage which was going off in the train we had left, when Holmes plucked my sleeve.

"Look," he said.

Far away, among the Kentish woods, there rose a thin spray of smoke, and hardly had we found a hiding place behind a pile of luggage, when the special train passed, with a rattle and a roar, beating a blast of hot air into our faces.

"There he goes," said Holmes. "For once, we have been a little too sharp for him."

"Suppose he had overtaken us, Holmes?"

"Oh, he would have tried to murder me. But that is not worth considering at this point. The question now is, shall we have lunch here, or wait till we arrive at Newhaven?"

That night we were in Brussels, and there we stayed for three days. Then we moved on to Strasburg, and on the Monday morning Holmes telegraphed to the London police. The reply came through in the evening, and Holmes tore it open, then with a bitter curse, hurled it into the fire.

"I might have known it," he groaned, "he has escaped."

"Moriarty?"

"They have secured the whole gang, with the exception of him. He has given them the slip. Well, I think you had better return to England, Watson."

"Why?"

"Because I am too dangerous a companion for you. This man is now quite desperate. He can never return to London, and it only remains for him to make the last supreme effort to finish me off. You had better go home, Watson."

I looked at him and smiled. I think he knew from the first that it was no use, that I should never desert so old a friend, especially now that he was in the greatest danger of his life. No, we would take what came together, and I told him so. That night we left for Geneva.

It was a charming week. We followed the lovely valley of the Rhone, enjoying the superb scene before us. The dainty green of the spring was fresh against the virgin white of the winter above. But Holmes never forgot that he was followed by a dark shadow. Every face we met he subjected to a quick glance and as we passed through Alpine villages or climbed the lonely mountain passes, I knew that he never expected to outwalk his enemy.

Once, as we passed over the Gemmi Pass, walking the border of the melancholy Lake Daubensee, a large rock, which had been dislodged from the ridge, clattered down and roared into the lake behind us. In an instant, Holmes raced up onto the ridge, and standing on a lofty pinnacle, craned his neck in every direction. It was in vain that our guide assured him that a fall of stones was a common thing in the springtime in that spot. Holmes said nothing, but I knew by his smile that he did not think the incident a matter of chance. He knew it was only another of Moriarty's failures.

But he was not depressed. He was gay and high-spirited. I think he thoroughly enjoyed the chase, with its ever-present sense of danger that acted like a tonic to his tired nerves. He talked enthusiastically of retiring when this case should be concluded.

"I am tired of criminal cases, Watson. I should like a chance to look into the problems of nature, for those that are caused by our artificial state of society no longer interest me. When I have Moriarty jailed, you can close your book of the adventures of Sherlock Holmes, and give your whole attention to your patients."

There is not much more to tell. I shall be brief, for I am now approaching the painful part of my story.

It was on the third of May that we reached the little village of Meiringen, where we put up at the English Inn. Our landlord spoke excellent English, having worked for three years in a London hotel. He advised us to take a trip to the little hamlet of Rosenlui, and on no account to miss seeing the wonderful Reichenbach Falls, which are halfway up the hills.

What a fearful place that is! A swollen torrent, full of melting snow, plunges into a tremendous abyss* and joins the river, which hurls itself into a glistening coal-black shaft, a creaming, boiling pit of great depth that chills the blood as one looks down into it, far below. One becomes dizzy with leaning over the edge watching the long sweep of green water roaring forever down, and the thick, flickering curtain of spray hissing forever upward. The noise is deafening and a half-human shout seems to come from the black depths below.

There is only a one-way path leading round the curve, and the traveler has to return by the way he came. Just as we turned back, a young Swiss lad came running along it with a letter in his hand. It was for me. I tore it open and read a message, written on the hotel paper by the landlord. It appeared that an English lady, in the last stages of tuberculosis, had been taken very ill, and the services of a doctor were needed at once. She refused to see a Swiss doctor, and since she was evidently dying, the kindly landlord felt that the presence of an English doctor might comfort her in her last hours.

*abyss: a deep cleft between high rocks.

I could not ignore such an appeal. I looked at Holmes. I could not help feeling troubled at the thought of leaving him alone in this deserted spot, but he seemed in no immediate danger. I decided to return with the young Swiss boy, while Holmes said he would remain a little while longer at the falls, then go slowly on to Rosenlui where I was to join him that night.

As I turned away, I saw Holmes, with his back against a rock and his arms folded, gazing down at the rush of waters. Little did I think that it was the last I was ever to see of him in this world.

When I was near the bottom of the descent, I looked back, but I could not see the falls, only the curving path which winds over the shoulder of the hill, and leads to it. Along this path was a man, I remember, walking very rapidly. I could see his black figure clearly outlined against the green behind him. I noted him and the speed with which he walked, but my mind was on my errand, and thinking no more of it, I hurried on to the inn.

In a little over an hour, I reached Meiringen, and the first person I saw, standing at the porch of the hotel, was the landlord.

"How is she?" I asked, hurrying up. "I trust she is no worse."

At his blank look, my heart turned to lead. In an instant, I knew we had been tricked. The letter, written upon hotel stationery, was a fake.

In a tinge of fear, I raced down the village street, making for the path I had so lately descended. But it was two hours before I reached the falls of Reichenbach once more. There was Holmes's alpenstock* leaning against the rock by which I had left him. But, shout as I would, there was no sign of Holmes himself. He was gone.

As I stared at the alpenstock, I felt sick. Then he had not gone on to Rosenlui. Instead, he had turned onto that narrow little one-way path overhanging those awful falls, where there was a sheer wall on one side, and a sheer drop on the other. And the man I had seen hurrying up the mountain path could have been none other than Moriarty himself. The young Swiss had disappeared. He must have been one of Moriarty's agents who, having done his work, had left the two men together. What had happened then? Who was to tell us that?

Dazed with horror, I stood, trying to pull myself together and to collect my thoughts. Then as my mind cleared of its first horrid shock, I began to apply Holmes's own methods, and to look carefully about me.

There was the alpenstock, marking the place where we had stood. The blackish soil is kept quite soft by the incessant spray, and a bird would leave its footmark upon it. I traced the two lines of footprints clearly along the edge of the footpath, both leading away from me. There were none returning.

Then a few yards from the end, the soil was all plowed up into a patch of mud, and the brambles and fern which

---

*alpenstock: a stout stick for mountain climbing.

fringed the edge were all torn and dragged. Here the struggle had taken place.

I lay upon my face and peered over, with the spray spouting up all around me. It had darkened since I left, and now I could see here and there only the glistening of moisture upon the black walls, and far away down at the end of the shaft the gleam of the broken water. I shouted, but only that half-human cry of the falls was borne back to my ears.

I looked sadly back at the alpenstock and there a gleam of something bright caught my eye. It was his silver cigarette case and as I picked it up from the boulder where it lay, the small square of paper that had been held down by its weight fluttered to the ground. Unfolding it, I found it addressed to me. On three pages torn from his notebook, I saw the familiar handwriting. The words were precise, and the writing

quite firm. It might have been written in his study, instead of on the edge of a raging waterfall, with certain death standing at his elbow. It read:

My Dear Watson:

I write these few lines through the courtesy of Mr. Moriarty, who awaits my convenience to finish the business that lies between us. He has been giving me a brief account of the means by which he avoided the London police and kept himself informed of our movements. I am still of the opinion that he is an extremely clever man.

I am pleased to think that I shall be able to free the world of his presence, though I fear it will be at a cost that will give pain to my friends, and especially, my dear Watson, to you. I have already explained to you that I felt my work had reached its climax and that I could find no better way to end it than this one.

Before I close, I must confess that I knew the letter from the landlord was a hoax and I allowed you to depart, knowing full well that something like this would happen. Tell Inspector Patterson that the papers he needs to convict the gang are in the pigeonhole M done up in a blue envelope and labeled "Moriarty."

I made all arrangements concerning my property before I left England and handed it over to my brother Mycroft. And now believe me, my dear fellow,

Very sincerely yours,
Sherlock Holmes

There is not much more to tell. Experts examined the scene by the falls and were convinced that Holmes and Moriarty, locked in their final struggle, had gone over the edge and had fallen to their deaths together. It was absolutely hopeless to attempt to discover their bodies, and there, deep down in that dreadful whirlpool of bubbling water, will lie for all time the most dangerous criminal and the foremost champion of the law of their generation. The Swiss youth was never found again, for he had vanished completely.

As to the gang, Holmes had completely exposed their organization, and the hand of the dead man weighed heavily upon them indeed. So little concerning their terrible chief, Moriarty, came out in the trials, that I felt it my duty to acquaint the world with the true facts.

I did this to clear the memory of attacks upon a man whom I shall ever regard as the best and wisest I have ever known.

The Return of Sherlock Holmes

My close intimacy with Sherlock Holmes had interested me deeply in crime, and after his disappearance I followed with care the various criminal cases in the papers. I even attempted to apply the methods of my famous friend to their solution, but never with much success.

It was the spring of 1894. I had been puzzling over the details of a tragic affair which was called in all the papers the Park Lane Mystery, and as evening drew on, I decided to go to the scene of the crime and have a look around. Accordingly, I strolled across the park, and at about six o'clock I reached the Oxford Street end of Park Lane. Among a group of loafers a tall, thin man, who looked like a plain-clothes detective, was explaining his theory of the murder of the Honorable Ronald Adair, and I joined the crowd to listen. His remarks struck me as foolish, and I backed away to leave.

As I did so, I struck against an elderly, deformed man who had been standing behind me, and I knocked down several of the books he was carrying. I stooped, picked them up, and started to apologize for the accident. With a snarl of contempt, the old man turned on his heel, and I saw his curved back and white side whiskers disappear among the throng.

I loitered for a few moments on the fringe of the small crowd, but could learn nothing, so I retraced my steps to my place at Kensington. I had not been in my study five minutes when a maid entered to say that a person wished to see me. To my astonishment, it was none other than the strange old book collector, his sharp withered face peering out from among a shock of white hair, and his precious volumes, a dozen of them at least, wedged under his arm.

"You're surprised to see me, sir," he said in a strange croaking voice.

"I am," I said.

"Well, I've a conscience, and as I chanced to see you go into this house, I just said to myself that I would step in and see that kind gentleman, and tell him that if I was a bit gruff in my manner, I meant no harm, and that I am grateful to him for picking up my books."

"It is nothing at all," I replied. "But tell me, how did you know who I was?"

"Well, sir, if it's not too great a liberty, I might say that I am a neighbor of yours and I keep a little bookshop at the corner of Church Street, and I should be very happy to see you there, I am sure. That gap on the second shelf there," pointing to my book shelves, "it looks rather untidy, doesn't it? Five books would just nicely fill the space."

I moved my head to look at the cabinet behind me. When I turned again, Sherlock Holmes was standing smiling at me from across my study table. I rose to my feet and stared at him for some seconds, and then I remember nothing more.

I must have fainted for the first and last time in my life. When the gray mist cleared away, I found my collar open and the tingle of brandy upon my lips, and bending over me, flask in hand, was Holmes.

"My dear Watson," said the well-remembered voice, "I owe you a thousand apologies. I had no idea you would be so affected."

I gripped him by the arms.

"Holmes!" I cried. "Is it really you? Are you really alive? How on earth did you succeed in climbing out of that awful abyss?"

"Gently, gently," he said, smiling. "You have had rather a shock. One thing at a time. I am so confoundedly dramatic, I fear I have overdone it this time."

"I am all right," I said. "But Holmes, I can hardly believe my eyes. Good heavens, to think that you—you, of all men—should actually be standing in my study." Again I gripped him and felt beneath my hand the thin, muscular arm. "Well, you're not a ghost, anyhow. My dear chap, I'm overjoyed to see you. Now sit down, and tell me everything."

He sat opposite to me and lit a cigarette in his old jaunty manner. He was dressed in the seedy frockcoat of the book merchant, but the rest of his disguise lay with the white hair and the books on my table. He looked thinner than of old, and there was a white tinge to his sharp face that told me his life of late had not been a healthy one. He stretched out his long legs.

"I am glad to stretch myself. It is no joke when a tall man has to take a foot off his height for several hours on end. Now, my dear fellow, before I give you an account of myself, let me ask you if you are willing to come with me tonight. There is hard and dangerous work ahead."

"When you like, and where you like."

"Ah, this is like the old days. We shall have time for a mouthful of dinner before we start. And about the abyss. I had no trouble getting out of it for the very simple reason that I never was in it."

"What? You never were in it?"

"No, Watson, I never was in it. My note to you was absolutely genuine, and I had no doubt that I had come to the

end of my career when I saw the sinister figure of the late
Professor Moriarty standing upon the narrow path that led
to safety. I could read his purpose in his gray eyes, and after
a few remarks I obtained his permission to write the note you
afterwards found.

"I left the note with my alpenstock and cigarette case,
then walked along the pathway, Moriarty at my heels. Then
I turned and stood at bay. He rushed at me and threw his
long arms about me. He knew that his own game was up,
and was only anxious to revenge himself upon me. We
tottered together on the brink of the falls, and for a bit I
thought it was all up with me.

"But I have some knowledge of baritsu, the Japanese
system of wrestling, and I slipped through his grasp, at the
same time throwing him off balance. With a horrible scream,
he fell, kicking madly, and clawing the air with his hands. I
saw him fall, a long, long way. Then he struck a rock,
bounced off, and splashed into the water."

I stared at him in amazement, while he calmly continued
to puff on his cigarette.

"But the tracks!" I cried. "I saw, with my own eyes,
that two went down the path and none returned."

"It came about in this way, Watson. As soon as I could
get my breath and recover myself, I realized what a lucky
chance fate had placed in my way. I knew that with the
death of Moriarty, I still was not safe. There were at least
three men who had sworn to destroy me, and with their
leader dead, they would be all the more determined to get
me. I thought that if they believed me dead, they would
play a bold hand, lay themselves open to the police, and
eventually would be trapped. Then when I was sure they
were all accounted for, I could return to the land of the
living. I thought all this out before the body of Professor
Moriarty had reached the bottom of the Reichenbach Falls.

"I stood up and examined the rocky wall behind me.
In your account of my death which I read with some interest

later, you said that the face of this rock was sheer. That is not quite true. There were a few small footholds, and up them I carefully climbed. It was not a pleasant climb, Watson, for the falls roared beneath me, and though I am not a fanciful man, I give you my word, Watson, I seemed to hear Moriarty's voice screaming at me out of the abyss below. A mistake would have been fatal. More than once, I almost fell, as tufts of grass came loose in my hands. Finally I reached a ledge where I could lie unseen and watch what happened on the path below."

"Then you must have been there all the time?"

"So I was, my dear Watson, and it took all my self-control to remain quiet. I watched you from above as you made your investigations, and followed your figure as it rounded the bend and went down the mountain. But as I crouched there again quite alone, or so I thought, a huge rock came bounding past me, struck the path and bounded

into the abyss below. For an instant, I thought it must have been an accident. Then, glancing up, I just caught a glimpse of a man's head against the darkening sky, and another stone struck the ledge where I lay, not a foot from my head."

"So someone knew I was still alive. I lost no time, Watson, after seeing that grim face look over the cliff, in scrambling down onto the path. It was dreadful, but I had no time to think of the danger. I landed, torn and bleeding, and took to my heels, did ten miles over the mountains in the darkness, and a week later was in Florence. By this time, I was sure that no one knew what had become of me."

"Then no one has heard from you since?"

"Well, to be honest with you, my dear Watson, I did take my brother Mycroft into my confidence. I could not reveal myself to you, of all persons, who had written so convincing an account of my death. Oh, I admit, several times during the past three years, I have taken up my pen to write to you. But I was afraid that in your concern you might accidentally do something that would tip off my enemies. I had to confide in Mycroft, to obtain the money I needed."

"And where have you been these past three years?"

"I have traveled in Tibet and spent some time with the High Lama in Lhasa. For some time, I worked under the name of a Norwegian explorer, Sigerson, of whom you must have read. I passed through Persia, stopped off at Mecca, visited in Egypt, and then returned to the Continent. I became interested in coal-tar products, and spent some time in a laboratory in the south of France. It was only recently that I learned that all but one of my enemies had been accounted for, that this last one was in London.

"Since I had become interested in the murder of the Honorable Ronald Adair, which the papers call the Park Lane Mystery, I thought I might return to London. So I came over at once, went to Baker Street, threw Mrs. Hudson into violent hysterics, and found myself wishing that the other armchair in my sitting room contained my old friend, Doctor Watson."

Then he smiled at me and leaned back in his chair. And this was the strange story that I listened to on that spring evening in 1894. I still stared unbelievingly at the tall thin figure and keen face of my old friend, whom I had thought never to see again.

Suddenly he sat up and put out his cigarette. "And now," he said briskly, "I have a piece of work for us both tonight, Watson, which, if we can bring it to a successful conclusion, will make us believe that we have not lived in vain."

I begged him to tell me more.

"No, not a word," said he. "Instead, let us talk of the past three years. We have till half-past nine. Then, and not till then, we shall embark on the adventure of the empty house."

The Adventure
of the Empty House

It was just like old times when at half-past nine, I took my seat beside Holmes in a hansom, my revolver in my pocket, and the thrill of adventure in my heart. Holmes was cold and stern and silent. As I caught glimpses of his tight, drawn face in the light of the street lamps, I knew not what beast we were tracking down in the dark jungle of criminal London, but I knew the adventure was a serious one—one of the most deadly serious we had ever embarked upon.

I thought we were bound for Baker Street, but Holmes stopped the cab at the corner of Cavendish Square. We got out, and followed a roundabout way to our destination. Holmes took the utmost care to see that we were not followed, and kept a sharp lookout in all directions. At last we entered a narrow, gloomy street, passed through a wooden gate into a deserted yard. Holmes drew a key from his pocket and opened the back door of a house. We entered, and he closed the door softly behind us.

The place was pitch dark, but I felt we were in an empty house. The bare floor creaked beneath out feet, and as I stretched out a hand to the wall, I could feel the paper hanging in ribbons. Holmes's cold thin fingers closed round my wrist, and we turned into a large, square, empty room, full of shadows, and lighted only from the street lamps outside.

Putting his lips close to my ear, he whispered, "Do you know where we are?"

"Why, in Baker Street," I answered, staring across out of the window.

"Exactly. We are in Camden House, which stands opposite to our old quarters."

"But why are we here?"

"Because from here, we can see everything over there. Draw a little closer to the window and look up at our old rooms. Tell me what you see."

I crept forward and looked at the familiar window. I gasped. The blind was down, and a strong light was burning in the room, and there, sharply etched against the light, was the perfect shadow of a man, seated in a chair at the window. The face was half turned round, and the whole presented a perfect silhouette of Holmes. I threw out my hand to make sure that the real Holmes stood beside me.

He exploded into silent laughter. "Well?" said he.

"It is astounding," I whispered back. "I should have taken it for you anywhere."

"Yes, it is rather like me, is it not?"

"I could swear it was you."

"I had it done by a French artist who took days in the modeling. It is a bust in wax. The rest I arranged myself this afternoon, when I so astonished Mrs. Hudson by my sudden appearance."

"But why?"

"Because, my dear Watson, I had the strongest motive for wishing certain people to think that I was there when I was really elsewhere."

"And you thought your rooms were watched?"

"I *knew* the rooms were watched."

"By whom?"

"By my old enemies, Watson. By the men who worked with that criminal whose body lies in the Reichenbach Falls. You must remember they were the only people who knew I was still alive. Sooner or later they knew I must return to my rooms in Baker Street. Accordingly, they watched them night and day, and this morning, they saw me arrive."

"How do you know?"

"Because I recognized their watchman. He is a harmless enough fellow, a strangler by trade, and he plays the jew'sharp very well. He did not bother me. It was the man behind him with whom I was concerned. That was the man who dropped the rocks over the cliff, and he is the most cunning and dangerous criminal in London. That is the man who is after me tonight, and that is the man who does not know that we are after *him*."

So in silence we stood together in the darkness, and watched the angular shadow on the blind in the window opposite, and the hurrying figures in the street outside. Holmes was silent and motionless, but his keen eye did not miss a thing.

It was a bleak and windy night, and many people were scurrying about. It seemed to me that there were two men in particular who appeared to be sheltering themselves from the wind in the doorway of a house up the street. I plucked Holmes's sleeve, but he shook me off with an impatient exclamation. As midnight approached, he began to pace up and down. Evidently, his plans were not working out as he expected.

Suddenly I noticed something. Again I clutched Holmes's arm and pointed upward.

"The shadow has moved!" I cried.

It was indeed no longer in profile, but now had its back to us.

Holmes frowned irritably. "Of course it has moved," he said. "Am I such an idiot as to erect a silly dummy and expect the sharpest men in Europe to be fooled by it? We have been in this room two hours, and Mrs. Hudson has made some change in that figure eight times, or once every quarter of an hour. She works it from the front so that her shadow may never be seen." Then he drew in his breath. "Ah!"

He was rigid with attention, his whole body leaning forward eagerly. I looked out too, but the street appeared absolutely deserted. If the two men were still crouched in the doorway up the street, they were not to be seen. Suddenly Holmes dragged me back into the darkest corner of the room, and I felt his warning hand upon my lips. His fingers were quivering, and never had I known him to be so excited. The street still stretched dark and empty before us.

Then I heard a sound which froze my blood. I felt Holmes grow tense at my side. The slight noise that came to my ears could mean only one thing. Someone had opened and shut a door in the back of the house. Steps meant to be silent crept down the passage. Holmes crouched back against the wall, and I did the same, my hand closing on my revolver. Peering through the gloom, I saw the dark shape of a man standing for an instant in the open door. As he crept forward, I braced myself to meet his spring.

But he must have had no idea that we were there, for he passed within three feet of us and went to the window, which he softly opened for about half a foot. He sank down to this level, and the light from the street showed us his face. He seemed to be wild with some inner excitement, for his eyes glittered and his face was twitching. We could see that it was deeply scored with savage lines. He was an elderly man with a great ragged mustache and a high bald front to his head on which he wore a silk hat tilted backward. As his overcoat fell open we saw the gleaming shirt front of a tuxedo.

I watched him, fascinated by what he was doing. He seemed to have in his hand a stick, but when he put it down, it rang like metal. Then from his overcoat pocket he drew a bulky object, and worked at something we could not see. A loud click, and then as he knelt there, he threw all his weight on some lever and I heard a whirling, grinding noise, and then another strong click. As he straightened up, I saw that in his hand was a sort of bulky gun which he opened at the breech, put something in, and snapped the lock shut. Then, crouching down again, he rested the end of the barrel on the window ledge, and cuddled the butt into his shoulder, as he trained his sights on the figure of Holmes in the lighted window.

His finger tightened on the trigger, and there was a strange, loud whizz and a silvery tinkle of broken glass. In an instant,

Holmes hurled himself onto the unsuspecting man and bore him to the floor. The fellow was up immediately and at Holmes's throat, but I struck him on the head with the butt of my revolver. As he dropped, I fell upon him, and pinned him down, while my comrade blew a shrill call on a whistle.

A clatter of running feet, and two policemen with one plain-clothes detective rushed through the front entrance and into the room.

"Is that you, Lestrade?" said Holmes.

"Yes, Mr. Holmes. I took this job myself. It's good to see you back in London, Mr. Holmes."

"I think you need a little unofficial help. Three unsolved murders in one year won't do, Lestrade."

Our prisoner, now breathing hard, was in the grip of the two policemen, and a small crowd gathered outside. Holmes stepped up to the window, closed it, and drew down the blind. Then Lestrade produced two candles, the policemen uncovered their lanterns, and we had a good look at the prisoner.

He was a fitting associate for the late Professor Moriarty. A great intellectual-looking forehead was his one good feature; the rest of the face was cruel and evil beyond words. He glared fiercely at Holmes.

"You fiend," he kept on muttering. "You clever, clever fiend."

"Ah, Colonel," said Holmes, arranging his rumpled collar. "I don't think I have had the pleasure of seeing you since you favored me with those little attentions as I lay on the ledge above the Reichenbach Falls."

The colonel still stared like a man in a trance.

"Permit me to introduce you gentlemen. This is Colonel Sebastian Moran, once of Her Majesty's Indian Army, and the best heavy-game shot that our Eastern Empire has produced. You still hold the tiger-shooting record, do you not, Colonel?"

The fierce old man, who looked not unlike a tiger himself, said nothing.

"I wonder that so old and experienced a hunter could be caught by my simple trap," went on Holmes. "I confess, I did not expect you would make use of this empty house and this convenient window. I expected you to operate from the street where Inspector Lestrade and his merry men were awaiting you. But, all's well that ends well."

With a snarl of rage, Colonel Moran sprang forward, but the policemen dragged him back.

"You may have a case against me," he told the inspector, "but there's no reason why I should have to listen to the sneers of this man. The law has me, and let the law deal with me."

"That's about right," said Lestrade. "Anything further you have to say, Mr. Holmes?"

But Holmes was lost in admiration of the powerful airgun, which he had picked up from the floor and now held in his hand.

"An admirable and most unusual weapon; noiseless, and of tremendous power. I knew the blind German mechanic who made this to the order of the late Professor Moriarty. I have waited years to handle it. Look at it, Lestrade, and don't forget the bullets that fit it."

"We'll take care of it, Mr. Holmes," said Lestrade. They moved toward the door. "Anything more?"

"What charge are you going to bring against Colonel Moran?"

"What charge, sir? Why, the attempted murder of Mr. Sherlock Holmes. What else?"

"Never mind me, Lestrade. I do not propose to appear in the case. I should suggest you charge the colonel with the murder of the Honorable Ronald Adair. The man you have there is the criminal that your whole force is seeking."

"What?"

"Yes. Your man, Colonel Sebastian Moran, shot Adair with an expanding bullet from an airgun, aimed through the open second-floor window of No. 427 Park Lane on the thirtieth of last month. That's the charge, Lestrade. And now, Watson, if you can endure the draft from my broken study window, let us go across the way and see what has happened to my double."

Our old rooms had been left unchanged in the absence of Holmes, thanks to Mycroft and Mrs. Hudson. The only difference was the fact that they were unusually tidy, a thing they never were when Holmes was living in them. There was the acid-stained old table on which he puttered through his endless experiments. There were the reference books and the scrapbooks which contained so many dangerous facts. There were the diagrams, the pipe-rack, and even the old Persian slipper in which Holmes kept his tobacco. And awaiting us was Mrs. Hudson. On the table stood the wax dummy of Sherlock Holmes.

It was a perfect likeness. It stood on a sort of small pedestal draped round with an old dressing gown of Holmes's.

"I hope you were careful, Mrs. Hudson," said he.

"I went to it on my knees, sir, just as you told me."

"Excellent. You did it very well. Did you see where the bullet went?"

"Yes, sir. I'm afraid it has ruined your beautiful bust, for it passed right through the head and flattened itself on the wall. Here it is."

"Ah, a soft revolver bullet, Watson, as you see. Who but a genius would think of firing such a thing from an airgun? Many thanks, Mrs. Hudson, for your valuable assistance."

We sat down, and Holmes, having discarded the seedy old frockcoat, wore once more the mouse-colored dressing gown that had adorned the bust.

"The old hunter's hand has not lost its cunning," he laughed, as he inspected the shattered forehead of the bust. "Plumb in the middle of the head and smack through the brain. Have you ever heard of Moran before?"

"No, I have not."

"Well, well. If I remember right, you had not heard the name Moriarty till I told you of it. And he had one of the great brains of the country. Let me see, now. Hand me that biography index, will you?"

I reached down his scrapbook and passed it over.

"Ah, the M's are a fine collection," he said. "Moriarty, the greatest of them all, then Morgan the poisoner, and the horrible Merridew, and Mathews, who knocked out my left eye-tooth in that waiting-room, and ah, yes, here, at last, is Moran."

I took the book from his hand and read the facts about Colonel Moran. He might have enjoyed a most brilliant and honorable army career. Instead, he had gone hopelessly wrong. In the margin opposite the vital facts concerning him was the notation in Holmes's neat script:

The second most dangerous man in London

"What a pity," I said, as I handed it back. "He is well born and well connected."

"Ah, yes. Up to a certain point, he did well. Then something must have snapped in that brain of his. Why, that man had an iron nerve, and they tell a story of his crawling down a drain pipe after a wounded man-eating tiger. Too bad." Holmes shook his head. "It seems it began with some scandal. Then India grew too hot to hold him, so he retired from the army and came to London. For some time he was chief of Moriarty's staff, and the professor supplied him with plenty of money and used him only for high-class jobs. This Moran is at the bottom of a number of crimes which no ordinary criminal could have performed."

I nodded.

"He kept himself cleverly concealed after the Moriarty gang broke up, but I knew he was here, lying in wait for me. Remember when I closed your shutters on that night before we went abroad? You probably thought me foolish, but I knew then about this airgun and that Moran, one of the world's great shots, was stalking me. He was also with us in Switzerland, and gave me those evil five minutes on that mountain ledge."

"But what attracted you to the murder of Ronald Adair?"

"Ah, yes, Ronald Adair. I was in the habit of watching the papers closely while abroad, and the facts in this case were unusually interesting. Knowing what I did, I felt sure that my chance had come at last. Was it not certain that Colonel Moran had done it? He had played cards with the lad, he had followed him home from their club, he had shot him through the open window. There was not a doubt of it. I lost no time in coming over to London and in allowing myself to be seen by the sentinel that Moran had posted near my rooms."

"Of course the bullets that killed Adair will connect Moran with the case now," I observed.

"Precisely. As to our success of tonight, I knew that when Moran learned of my arrival in London, he would connect my return with his crime and be terribly alarmed. For his own sake, he would have to murder me as soon as possible. So I notified the police, set my trap, and the rest was easy."

"But what was Colonel Moran's motive for murdering young Adair?"

"I have only a theory, Watson, but I think it is as good as any, and is probably quite correct. It came out in the evidence that Colonel Moran and young Adair had between them won a considerable sum of money. Moran undoubtedly cheated, and Adair must have discovered this on the day of his death. He must have warned Moran that he would expose his foul playing unless he resigned at once from the club and promised not to play cards again. This Moran could not afford to do, for with Moriarty dead, he was reduced to making his living by cheating at cards."

"It all sounds reasonable."

"I think so. He murdered Adair at the very moment when the young man was counting out his share of the money that he meant to return, since he was too honorable to profit by his partner's cheating. You recall that he had locked himself in his room, lest his family come in and wonder what he was doing with all that money in piles on his table. Will it pass?"

"I think you have, as usual, hit upon the truth."

"Well, it will all come out in the trial. At any rate, Colonel Moran will trouble us no more, and the famous airgun will become a feature of the Scotland Yard Museum and as for Mr. Sherlock Holmes—"

"What about him?" I smiled.

"I suppose he will go back to solving crimes. Evidently the time has not yet come for him to retire."

The Adventure of the Priory School

One morning Mrs. Hudson brought us the card of a visitor. On it, we read, "Thorneycroft Huxtable, M.A., Ph.D.," and in a moment the gentleman himself appeared. He was a large, important-looking person, dignified and solid, but before we could get out a word of greeting, he staggered and fell all his length in a dead faint upon our bearskin rug.

We sprang to action, I to get some brandy and Holmes to slip a cushion under the heavy head. The man's face was deathly white and scored with deep lines of trouble. Dark circles marked his closed eyes, and his rolling chins were unshaved. His clothes were crushed and his shirt was soiled, his hair was rumpled, and altogether, he was a sorry sight.

"He is absolutely exhausted, but I fancy he will be all right with rest and care," I said, as I kept my finger on his fluttering pulse. Holmes drew from the watch pocket a railway ticket, which showed that the man had come from Mackleton, in the north of England.

"It is not twelve o'clock yet. He must have started very early," said Holmes.

By now our visitor was stirring, and soon opened his dull eyes. He flushed crimson, and staggered to his feet.

"I am sorry for this, Mr. Holmes, but I have been a little over-strained. If I might have a glass of milk and a biscuit— I think I should be all right. I came myself, fearing that a telegram would be of no use in the matter."

Holmes shook his head. "I am afraid that you have come at a bad time, sir, for both Dr. Watson and myself are deep in another case. We can give you no time at all."

"But you must listen to me!" cried our visitor desperately. "This is no ordinary matter, I assure you. We have done our best to keep it out of the papers, but last night the *Globe* published a rumor. Perhaps you saw it. The son of the Duke of Holdernesse—"

"Just a minute." Holmes shot out a long thin arm and took down a reference volume labeled H. "Ah, yes, here we are. Hm." He read for a few moments in silence. "Yes. Quite a distinguished nobleman, the Duke of Holdernesse. And only one son, young Lord Saltire. You say the boy has disappeared?"

"I didn't. You must have read it in the paper. Yes, he has disappeared, and we are nearly frantic. The Duke has offered five thousand pounds to the man who can tell him where his son is, and another thousand to the man who can name the person or persons who have kidnapped him."

"That is a princely offer," said Holmes. There was a strained silence, while Dr. Huxtable sipped his glass of milk and tried to eat the biscuits brought him by Mrs. Hudson. Holmes stared at the ceiling, then looked at me.

"Perhaps, Watson, we ought to accompany Dr. Huxtable back to the north of England. When you have finished your milk, sir, perhaps you can inform us as to why Dr. Thorneycroft Huxtable, of the Priory School, near Mackleton, has waited three days before consulting us in such a serious matter as a kidnapping. You need not look surprised, sir. I can tell the date of Lord Saltire's disappearance by the condition of your chin."

Our visitor recovered from his shock, and as he finished his milk, he told us his story.

"I must inform you, gentlemen, that the Priory is a preparatory school. I am the founder and principal. Three weeks ago, a Mr. James Wilder, secretary to his Grace, the Duke of Holdernesse, came to enroll young Lord Saltire, ten years old, in the school.

"The lad arrived on May 1, for that was the beginning of the summer term. He was a very nice boy, but he seemed unhappy, more so than he would be if he were merely entering a new school where he felt strange. His mother and father had recently separated, and the duchess had gone to live in the south of France. The boy loved his mother dearly, and was so miserable after her departure that his father decided to send him to boarding school. In two weeks, however, he began to feel at home, and seemed quite contented.

"Then it happened. He was last seen on the night of May 13, that is, on the Monday. His room, on the second floor, opened out of a larger room, where two boys slept. These boys saw him go into his room, but did not see him come out, although they were there all the time. Apparently he had left by his window, which was open, and had climbed down a stout ivy vine that grew on the wall outside. Although there were no footsteps below the window, everyone felt sure that he had left by this means.

"He was fully dressed in his usual suit of black Eton jacket and dark gray trousers. There were no evidences of a struggle or sign that anyone had entered the boy's room."

Dr. Huxtable paused. His face had gone quite white again, and a slight perspiration glistened on his forehead. I give the remainder of the story in his own words.

"When we discovered Lord Saltire's disappearance, I at once summoned the whole school, boys, masters, and servants. It was then that we learned that the boy had not left alone. Heidegger, the German master, was also missing. He had left hurriedly, partly dressed, for we found his shirt and socks on his bedroom floor."

"How did he leave?" asked Holmes.

"By the same method. He let himself down by the ivy, for his foot marks were on the lawn. His bicycle, which he kept in a small shed nearby, was also gone."

"What sort of man was he?"

"He was a silent, sullen fellow, and no one liked him. However, he came to me two years ago, with the best of references, and I trusted him absolutely. The first thing we did was to go straight to Holdernesse Hall, which is a few miles away, thinking perhaps that the boy, in a sudden fit of homesickness, had gone to his father. But he was not there."

"I see. And the father, quite naturally, is dreadfully upset," said Holmes.

"Not more so than we ourselves. I am in a state of nervous prostration, as you can see. Mr. Holmes, you cannot refuse to help us."

Holmes, listening with the utmost concentration, jotted down a few notes in a little book.

"You are greatly to blame in not coming to me sooner." he said. "I am under a serious handicap by starting on my investigation so late. No doubt the ivy and the lawn have been quite spoiled for possible clues, for there have probably been police all over the place."

"Oh, yes. But I had to keep the thing as quiet as possible, for the duke has a horror of publicity and scandal."

"What have the police learned?"

"All we know is that a young boy and a man were reported leaving a neighboring station by an early train. We followed them to Liverpool, where they proved to be strangers. It was then that my despair drove me to you, Mr. Holmes."

In this way, three days had been lost, wasted, while the

police ran down a false clue. Holmes put short, sharp questions to the distracted schoolmaster, and learned that there was no apparent connection between the missing boy and the German teacher. So far as they knew, the doctor said that the boy had never exchanged a word with Heidegger. The boy himself had no bicycle, and there was none missing from the school. No one had called to see the boy on the day of his disappearance, and he had received only one letter, and that was from his father.

"How did you know this?" said Holmes. "Do you open the boys' letters?"

"No. But there was the coat of arms on the envelope and the letter was addressed in the duke's peculiar stiff handwriting."

No letter had come from France, either. Holmes was particular to make sure of that.

"How did you know that the boy's sympathies were with the mother?" asked Holmes. "Did the duke tell you that?"

"Good heavens, no. The duke is a very stiff and formal man, and would not dream of discussing his private affairs with a near stranger like myself."

"Then did the boy tell you?"

"No. I have had several confidential chats with Mr. James Wilder, the duke's secretary, and he told me of Lord Saltire's feelings."

"I see. Did the boy take his father's letter with him?"

"Yes. At least, we could not find it. I think, Mr. Holmes, it is time we were leaving for the station."

"We shall leave within a quarter of an hour. I think you should telegraph your people to let the chase continue to Liverpool, while I do a little quiet investigating on my own. Perhaps the scent is not so cold but that a pair of old hounds like Watson and myself can get a sniff of it."

We left at once for the north, and that evening we were in the cold bracing atmosphere of that bleak country. We were met at the door of the school by the butler who whispered to his master that the duke and Mr. Wilder were awaiting us in the study.

I was familiar with pictures of the famous statesman, but I was hardly prepared for the sight I now had of the tall, stately person, beautifully dressed, his face drawn and thin, and dominated by a long, curved nose. His skin was dead white, and this made his brilliant red beard seem all the more vivid. He stood on the hearthrug and stared coldly at us as we entered.

Mr. Wilder, a small nervous person, with an intelligent face and light-blue eyes, opened the conversation.

"His Grace is surprised, Dr. Huxtable, that you have gone to Mr. Sherlock Holmes without first consulting him. He is by no means convinced that the police have failed."

"But—" began the doctor.

"His Grace is particularly anxious to avoid scandal," went on Mr. Wilder.

"In that case," said Dr. Huxtable hastily, "Mr. Holmes can return to London first thing in the morning."

"I hardly think so, my good doctor," said Holmes sweetly. "I find this bracing northern air agrees with me. I propose to spend a few days upon your moors, and if I am in the way here, I can put up at the village inn."

"Not at all," boomed out the sudden voice of the duke. "Since we have gone this far, we shall continue. I should be pleased, Mr. Holmes, if you and your companion would come and stay with me at Holdernesse Hall."

"Although I may have to call upon you there, I think it wiser for me to remain at the scene of the mystery," said Holmes. "Thank you all the same, sir. Now, let me ask you, have you yourself formed any opinion as to the mysterious disappearance of your son?"

"No, sir, I have not."

"Excuse me if I ask you a question that may be painful to you. Do you think that the duchess had anything to do with the matter?"

The duke hesitated. "No, I do not think so," he said.

"Have you had any demand for ransom?"

"No, sir."

"Was there anything in the letter you wrote to your son on the day of his disappearance that might have caused him to leave the school?"

"No, sir, certainly not."

"Did you yourself mail the letter?"

Before the duke could reply, his secretary interrupted with some heat.

"His Grace is not in the habit of mailing letters himself," he said. "I myself attended to it when the other mail was sent off."

"For my own part," went on the duke, "I still do not think that the duchess would encourage the boy to do anything like this. But he had some wrong ideas, and it is possible that, with the aid of this German master, he had fled to her in France. I think I shall now return home, Dr. Huxtable. I believe we have done all we can do tonight."

I could see that the nobleman was upset at having to discuss his private family affairs with strangers, and was anxious to put an end to the interview. As for Holmes, as soon as the visitors had left, he flung himself headfirst into the case.

First he examined the boy's room carefully, and this strengthened the belief that the boy had certainly left through the window. The German master's room and belongings gave no further clue, except that a trailer of ivy had given way under his weight, and he had come down heavily on the lawn, leaving his track in the grass.

Sherlock Holmes left the school alone, and returned soon after eleven. With him he had a large map of the surrounding country which he laid out on the bed near the lamp, and over which he began to smoke, occasionally pointing out objects with the reeking amber mouthpiece of his pipe.

"This is a most unusual and interesting case, Watson,"

he said, after a time. "Now, look at this map. This dark square is the Priory School. Here is the main road running east and west past the school. I have learned that our two missing persons positively did not leave by this road."

"Oh, you have? But how?"

"Simply by learning that at the east end of the road there was a constable on duty all night. At the west end, the people of the Red Bull Inn were on the lookout all night for the doctor. The landlady was ill, and had anyone else been passing, the people in the inn could not have missed them."

"What about the country to the south of the road?"

"It is impassable, Watson. All small fields and stone walls. A bicycle could not get through. So that leaves only one direction for our two to take."

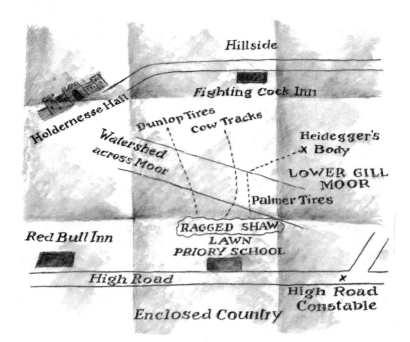

"The north," I said.

"Exactly."

"But the bicycle?"

"Patience. I am coming to that. Now, if our people went by the north—and that much is certain—they could easily find their way on any of the numerous paths, and . . . hello, what's this?"

There was a quick knock at the door, and in burst Dr. Huxtable, a blue cap in his hand.

"At last we have a clue!" he cried. "Thank Heaven! This is the dear boy's cap!"

"Where was it found?"

"In a gypsy van. They were camped on the moor last Tuesday. Today the police traced them down and questioned them. Of course they lied and shuffled, but they know where he is, all right. They are all under lock and key and the fear of the law will soon loosen their tongues."

With that, he left us.

"So far, so good," said Holmes. "At least, that bears out our theory, Watson, that it is on the side of Lower Gill Moor that we must hope for results. Now, see here, this is a watercourse, marked out as you see, and here and there it widens into a swamp. It is very bad between Holdernesse Hall and the school. There will be no tracks here in this dry weather, but *there* where all is damp and swampy, we shall surely find something. We shall start early in the morning."

The day was just breaking when I awoke to see Holmes, fully dressed, standing by my bedside. He had already been out.

"Come on, Watson. I have already done the lawn and the bicycle shed, and I had a ramble through the Ragged Shaw, that region of woods over there—" he pointed out of the window to the north. "Hurry, man, get your clothes on. There's a cup of hot cocoa in the next room, and then, let us be off!"

His eyes shone, and his whole form seemed eager and

alert. He was a very different person from the dreamy, quiet Holmes who would lie for hours on his sofa at Baker Street, staring at nothing, and saying not a word. Now he was flushed and full of energy.

We met with immediate disappointment. Sheep tracks and cow tracks, but no sign either of the boy or the German's having passed that way. With a darkening face, Holmes strode along, examining carefully every little stain or mark along the path. Nothing.

He stopped and stared gloomily out over the rolling moor. "Check," he muttered. "Nothing at all—wait! What have we here?"

We had come upon a small black ribbon of pathway. In the middle of it, clearly marked on the soaked soil, was the track of a bicycle.

"Hurrah!" I cried. "We have it!"

But Holmes shook his head. "A bicycle certainly, but not *the* bicycle. I am familiar with forty-two impressions of tires. This one is a Dunlop, with a patch upon the outer cover, whereas Heidegger's bicycle has Palmer tires which have long stripes running parallel with the tire. The mathematics teacher told me as much. No, this is not Heidegger's bicycle track."

"Perhaps it is the boy's, then?" I offered.

"Possibly, if we could prove the boy to have had a bicycle in his possession. However, this track was made by someone leaving the school. The deeper impression made by the hind wheel has frequently passed over the lighter front one. Well, this may or may not be important. Let us go backwards and trace the tracks."

We did so, and soon lost them at the edge of the boggy portion of the moor. Then we picked them up again, where they were nearly covered by the tracks of cows. The path now ran right onto the Ragged Shaw, and the track was again lost. Holmes sat down on a boulder, and rested his chin on his hands for quite some time.

"Well, well," he said at last. "There is always the possibility that the person who rode this bicycle with the Dunlop tires might have changed them to throw us off the scent. I should be proud to do business with so clever a criminal. Let us go back to the swamp, Watson."

We soon were rewarded. There, right across our path, was the unmistakable striped track of Palmer tires.

"Herr Hiedegger, sure enough!" cried Holmes. "My reasoning seems to be pretty sound, Watson."

"I congratulate you," I said.

"Kindly walk clear of the path. Let us get on."

We lost the tracks, picked them up again, and once again lost them. Finally they came out, deep and clear.

"Do you observe," said Holmes, "that the rider is now undoubtedly forcing himself? Look at the equal depth of the impressions. He must be throwing his weight on the handlebars as a man does when sprinting. By Jove! He's had a fall!"

There was a broad, irregular smudge, some footmarks, and then the tire tracks again.

"He only slipped," I said.

For answer, Holmes held up a crumpled branch of flowering shrub. To my horror I saw that the yellow blossoms were all dappled with blood. Both the path and the heather were also stained with dark blots.

"Bad!" said Holmes. "Bad! Don't step on the path, Watson. Now, what do I read here? He fell wounded—he stood up—he remounted—he went on. But there is another track. Ah, only the cattle. He was not gored by a wild bull! Impossible! Still, there are no other traces of anyone's being here. Come on, Watson, quick!"

We had not far to go. The tracks curved into a bush where we saw the gleam of handlebars. Out we dragged the bicycle, Palmer-tired, the whole front of it horribly smeared with blood. On the other side of the bushes, a shoe was projecting.

We ran round, and there lay the unfortunate rider. He

was a tall man, full-bearded, with broken spectacles, lying on his face. He had been killed by a frightful blow on the head which had crushed in part of his skull. How he could have gone as far as he did with such a wound is a mystery.

"He must have been a man of great vitality and courage," said Holmes as he gently turned the body over. The man wore shoes, but no socks, and under his coat was his nightshirt. It was undoubtedly the German master.

We sent a farmer who was cutting up peat* nearby to fetch the police, while we ourselves pushed on. Holmes was

*peat: a piece of turf used for fuel.

unwilling to leave the trail which had suddenly become hot. He remained gazing at the corpse of the unfortunate teacher.

"Yes," he murmured. "The body was fully dressed before he left his room, and from his own window, Heidegger saw the lad's flight. He at once climbed down, seized his bicycle, and followed hot on the boy's trail. In pursuing him, he met his death."

"So it would seem."

"Now. The man is killed five miles from the school. Not by a bullet, you will see, but by a savage blow dealt from a strong arm. That proves the lad had a companion in his flight. The flight must have been a swift one, since Heidegger did not attempt to overtake them on foot, and it took him, an expert cyclist, five miles to reach them.

"This tells us that the boy was not on foot. But how did the boy travel? All we find are cow tracks. There is no other path for fifty yards. What happened?"

"The whole thing is impossible." I said.

"Excellent, Watson. It *is* impossible, therefore my reasoning is at fault. What mistake have I made? Can you suggest one?"

"He could have fractured his skull in a fall."

"In a swamp, Watson? Impossible!"

"I am at my wit's end."

"Tut, tut, we have solved worse problems than this one. Let us go back to the track of the Dunlop tires and see if we have overlooked anything there."

This track led both to Holdernesse Hall, whose stately gray towers were near at hand, and to the low gray village, which lay in front of us on the way to the Chesterfield Road. There was a dirty inn with the sign of a gamecock swinging over its door. As we approached, Holmes gave a sudden groan, and clutched me by the shoulder. He had strained his ankle, and could hardly walk. In evident pain, he limped up to the door, where a thick-set, elderly man was smoking a dark clay pipe.

"How are you, Mr. Reuben Hayes?" he said.

"Who are you, and how do you know my name so pat?" the country man said with a suspicious flash in his shifty eyes.

"Well, it's printed on the board above your head, and it's easy to see a man who is master of his own house. Do you have such a thing as a carriage in your stables?"

"No, I have not."

"I can hardly put my foot to the ground."

"Don't put it to the ground."

"But I can't walk."

"Well, then, hop."

It was plain to see that the landlord of the Fighting Cock Inn was not going to help us. Holmes offered him a sovereign for the use of a bicycle. At this, the landlord pricked up his ears. When Holmes said he wanted to get to Holdernesse Hall, he was even more interested.

"So you're pals of the duke, are you?"

"I don't know about that," laughed Holmes. "But I know he'll be glad to hear that we are on the track of his lost son."

The landlord gave a start. Suddenly he became more friendly. "You wouldn't like to state where you think he is, would you?"

"Certainly. We have traced him to Liverpool," said Holmes.

"Well, I'm glad to hear of that," said the landlord. "I was once the duke's head coachman, and cruel bad he treated me. Fired me for no reason at all, he did. But I'm glad to hear good news of the young lord. I'll help you to get to the Hall."

Although the landlord had no bicycle, he offered us a couple of horses, and while they were being made ready, Holmes ordered some food. We awaited it in the flagstone kitchen, and when we were alone, it was astonishing how quickly Holmes's ankle recovered. It was close to nightfall and we were hungry, having eaten nothing since morning.

We lingered over our meal, Holmes saying very little as he ate.

Suddenly he sprang out of his chair.

"By Heaven, Watson, I believe I've got it! Yes, yes, it must be so! Do you remember those cow tracks, Watson?"

"Yes."

"Where were they?"

"Well, everywhere. They were at the swamp, on the path, and near where poor Heidegger met his death."

"Exactly. Now, Watson, tell me, how many cows did you see on the moor?"

"Why, none."

"Did that strike you as strange, Watson, that we should see tracks everywhere, but no cows to make those tracks?"

"Yes, it is strange, now that you mention it."

"Now, throw your mind back, Watson. Recall the position of those tracks."

"I cannot."

"Look!" cried Holmes excitedly, as he arranged some crumbs of bread on the table. "Now, some were like these ⋮ ⋮ ⋮ ⋮ and some were like these ⋰ ⋰ ⋰ ⋰ and then some were like this ⋯⋯⋯⋯ Can you remember that?"

"No, I cannot say that I do."

"I could swear to it, but we can go back and make sure. What a blind beetle I have been, Watson! It was so perfectly obvious."

"What was obvious, may I ask?"

"Well, is it not a remarkable cow that walks, canters, and gallops? Come, Watson, let us see if we can find this remarkable cow."

We made for the tumble-down stable, and there were two rough ill-kept horses. Holmes raised the hind leg of one of them and laughed aloud.

"What did I say? Here is your cow."

The horse wore its old shoes, to be sure, but it had been lately reshod, for the nails were bright and new. Holmes's eyes darted to and fro, as if searching for something in the litter of iron and wood on the floor.

Suddenly we heard a step behind us, and there was the landlord, his heavy eyebrows drawn over his savage eyes, and his face twisted with rage. He held a short, metal-headed stick in his hand, and he advanced toward us. I slipped my hand into my revolver pocket.

"You infernal spies!" he snarled. "What are you doing there?"

"Why, Mr. Reuben Hayes," said Holmes calmly. "Are you afraid of our finding something out?"

The man gave an uneasy laugh and cooled off. "I don't like folks poking around my smithy," he said. "Pay your bill, and get out."

"Gladly," said Holmes. "And I think we'll walk, after all. My ankle is feeling somewhat better. I presume it is not too far to Holdernesse Hall?"

"About two miles," said the landlord.

As soon as we were round the curve and hidden from sight of the inn, Holmes stopped.

"We were very warm at that inn just now, and I feel we are getting colder and colder as we get farther away. I think we'll stay, Watson."

"Yes, I think the landlord knows a good deal about the case," I said.

"So he impressed you that way also?" Holmes glanced rapidly around. "Let us return by a roundabout way, Watson." Then as we made our way up the hill, a solitary man on a bicycle could be seen approaching through the trees from the direction of the Hall. "Get down, Watson!" cried Holmes, with a heavy hand on my shoulder.

We sank behind some bushes only a moment before the cyclist was on us. Amid a rolling cloud of dust, I caught sight of a pale, frightened face, stiff with horror, the mouth open, the eyes wildly staring, as the man whirled past. It was Mr. James Wilder, the duke's young secretary.

"Come on, Watson!" cried Holmes, scrambling up. "Let's follow and see what he does!"

We stalked him carefully to the inn, where we saw his bicycle leaning against the front door. It was getting dark as the sun slowly sank behind the towers of Holdernesse Hall. Then we saw the sidelamps of a carriage light up the yard of the inn, and someone drove it off at a furious pace in the direction of Chesterfield.

"What do you make of that, Watson?" whispered Holmes.

"Looks as if someone were in a hurry to get away," I answered.

"A single man, so far as I could see. But it was not Mr. James Wilder, for there he is at the door."

A red square of light had sprung out of the darkness, and silhouetted against it was the slight figure of the secretary as he stood there, peering out into the night. He was obviously expecting someone. Then at last there were steps in the road, and he was joined by a second figure, the door was shut, and all was black once more. Five minutes later, a lamp was lit on an upper floor.

"Strange customers the Fighting Cock has," murmured Holmes.

"The bar is on the other side," I said.

"Quite so. Those are private guests from the look of them. Now, what in the world is Mr. James Wilder doing there, and who joined him?"

At his signal, I followed him past the front and round to the side of the inn. We stopped to view the bicycle that leaned against the door, and Holmes struck a light, bent down, and chuckled. It was the Dunlop tires with the patch on one side. Directly above us was the lighted window.

"I must have a peep in there, Watson. Can you bend down for a few minutes and let me climb on your back?"

In an instant his feet were on my back, but he was hardly up before he was down again.

"Come, my friend," he said, "our day's work has been quite long enough. It's a long walk to the school, and the sooner we get started, the better."

He would hardly open his lips again that night, and we trudged back to the Priory School in silence. He would not go in, but went on to the Mackleton Post Office where he sent a number of telegrams, and later, from my bedroom, I

heard him speaking to the shattered Dr. Huxtable about the death of the German master.

He came into my room to say good night. He was as alert and vigorous as when we started in the morning. "All goes well, my friend," said he. "I promise that before tomorrow morning, we shall have reached the solution of the mystery."

* * *

Now, my friends, what do *you* make of all this? Is the young son of the Duke of Holdernesse safe and well? What connection has Mr. James Wilder with the disappearance? And have you any theories as to the identity of the mysterious person who met Wilder at the Fighting Cock Inn? Holmes knows who it was, but apparently, he is not ready to tell even me.

Recall the finding of the cap in the gypsy caravan and see if you can fit that into the mystery. Do you feel that the duke is holding something back, that he might have another reason for wanting to avoid scandal? It may be that he fears that whoever has his son will kill him if there is too loud an outcry made.

Have you settled in your mind the cause of the German master's death? Certainly the new nails in the horses' shoes told Holmes something, and what he found in the dirty old stable gave him great satisfaction. What do you think it was? It was then, you recall, that Holmes began to feel that he would soon know the answer to the boy's disappearance.

Why did the duke hesitate when Holmes referred to the boy's mother? Do you think she has anything to do with the matter and that he is trying to shield her?

Well, we shall soon know the answer to all these questions, for I now resume my story.

* * *

At eleven o'clock the next morning, Holmes and I walked up the magnificent avenue of yews* to Holdernesse Hall. We went through an Elizabethan doorway and were shown into the duke's study. There we found Mr. James Wilder, who was quite composed now, although in his light-blue eyes there were still traces of the terror we had seen there on the previous night.

Mr. Wilder tried to prevent our seeing the duke, and excused his employer by saying that he was much upset over the tragic news of Heidegger's death. When Holmes coldly insisted, Wilder said the duke was still in bed.

But Holmes would not give way, and the secretary went up to the duke's bedroom. In about an hour the nobleman himself appeared, but he was sadly shaken up by the news of the previous day. His face was more shrunken, and his shoulders sagged. But he was courteous in greeting us, and sat down at his table, onto which his long, red beard streamed.

Holmes refused to speak until Wilder had gone, and at an order from the duke, the man left, after shooting an angry glance in our direction.

"Now," said Holmes briskly, "as to the reward. Dr.

*yew: a tall tree not unlike a poplar.

Huxtable said that a considerable sum had been offered for information regarding your son's whereabouts. I am now ready to claim that sum."

"It is true," said the duke stiffly, "that I have offered six thousand pounds in all for this information. Do your work well, Mr. Holmes, and you shall have no reason to complain of me."

"I have done the work, and your Grace may make out the check," said Holmes.

I was surprised, for Holmes was not usually greedy for money. He now rubbed his thin hands together and seemed entirely pleased with himself.

The duke looked astounded. "Is this a joke, Mr. Holmes?" he asked.

"Not at all, your Grace. I am in dead earnest," said Holmes. "I have earned the reward. I know where your son is and who is holding him."

The duke's beard flamed against the ghastly white of his face.

"Where is he?" he gasped.

"He is, or he was, last night, at the Fighting Cock Inn, about two miles from your park gate."

The duke fell back in his chair.

"And whom do you accuse?"

Sherlock Holmes's answer was an astounding one. Stepping forward swiftly, he touched the duke on the shoulder.

"I accuse *you*," he said. "And now, I'll trouble you for that check, please."

The duke sprang up, and with a death-like expression on his face, he fairly clawed the air as if sinking into a pit. Then he controlled himself, sat down, and sank his face into his hands.

"How much do you know?" he said at last, without raising his head.

"I saw you together last night. Do not fear. No one else has heard it from me."

The duke drew his checkbook toward him. He took up his pen in trembling fingers. "I shall be as good as my word, Mr. Holmes. I hardly expected things to turn out like this, but you and your friend are men who may be trusted, I think?"

"What do you mean?" said Holmes.

"There is no need for anyone else to know of this incident, Mr. Holmes. I believe the amount I owe you is twelve thousand pounds, is it not?"

But Holmes smiled and shook his head.

"I fear, your Grace, that matters cannot be arranged so easily. There is the death of this poor school teacher to be accounted for."

"But James knew nothing of that. You cannot hold him responsible for that. It was the work of the brutal ruffian he had the misfortune to employ."

"Ah, but it is not so simple as that, your Grace. James Wilder committed one crime. Another one was committed, a murder, and although he knew nothing of it, he is in part responsible for it."

"But James was not present at the murder and never expected so horrible a thing to happen. The law cannot try him for a murder that he did not plan nor commit."

"Well, well, we shall see," said Holmes.

"As soon as James heard of the death of Heidegger, he at once came to me, filled with horror, and confessed the whole thing. Oh, Mr. Holmes, you must save him! I tell you that you must save him!" The duke had again lost control of his emotions and was pacing the room, his face trembling and his eyes full of tears. Then he mastered himself, and once-more sat down. "We must think what to do."

"I realize that James Wilder is not the murderer, nor even the kidnapper," said Holmes.

"No, the murderer has escaped."

Holmes smiled. "Ah, it is not easy for anyone to escape

me, not so easy as you might think, your Grace. According to a telegram I received this morning from the head of the local police, Mr. Reuben Hayes was arrested at Chesterfield at eleven o'clock last night. So you see, his trip from the inn was a short one."

The Duke of Holdernesse stared in amazement at my friend.

"How do you do it?" he gasped. "Your powers are not human. However, I am glad he has been taken, that is, provided it does not drag James into the case."

"You seem unusually concerned for your secretary, your Grace."

"He is my son, sir."

It was Holmes's turn to look astounded. He knew there was a mystery here regarding the secretary, but I do not think it had ever crossed his mind that Wilder might be the duke's son.

"I will tell you all," said the duke. "There is no point in concealing it from you gentlemen now."

He sighed heavily and began.

"This whole tragedy has come about through James's folly and jealousy. He is my son by a lady I dearly loved, but who refused to marry me, since the marriage might ruin my career. I begged her to marry me, but she was firm. If she had lived, I should have insisted on marrying her, no matter what the cost. But she died, and left this one child, my son, who reminded me so much of her and her ways that I have cherished and cared for him all his life.

"For reasons which you will understand, I could not come out before the world as his father, but I have given him the finest of educations. Since he grew up, he has always been near me. I never told him who he really was, but one day he discovered for himself that I was his father. Since then, there has been no peace.

"He has bad blood in him, for all he is my son, and he

became furiously jealous of my young son, Arthur. James insisted that *he* should inherit the fortune, and it was his bad behavior that caused the duchess to leave and go to France. But still I could not bear to part from him, for he reminded me so strongly of his mother.

"He became friendly with Hayes, a low fellow whom I dismissed some time ago for stealing, and I knew they were plotting to do some mischief to young Arthur. That was why I placed him in the Priory School, where I felt sure he would be safe."

"You wrote to Arthur on that last day, did you not?" put in Holmes.

"I did. I wrote an ordinary note to my boy, and left it for James to post. I blame myself now for this. James opened the letter, inserted a note in it telling Arthur that his mother had secretly returned and was longing to see him. Poor Arthur fell into the trap. He readily went to meet James in the Ragged Shaw, expecting to be taken to where his mother awaited him. He left the school at midnight, and met, not James, but Hayes, with a pony. They set off together.

"But they were pursued by the German master, who feared for the boy's safety, and Hayes, in his rage and excitement, struck Heidegger down. Not knowing he had killed him, he then brought Arthur to the Fighting Cock Inn and gave him into the care of Mrs. Hayes, a kindly woman, but entirely under the influence of her evil husband."

"And this was the state of affairs when we met two days ago?" asked Holmes.

"It was. I had no more idea of the truth then than you. All that I have told you I have learned from James's confession. He intended to hold Arthur until I consented to break the will I had made, making him my heir, after which he would return my boy to me. It was discovery of Heidegger's body that spoiled the plans."

"And I suppose Wilder then rushed to warn Hayes that the man he had struck down was dead and the body discovered?"

"Yes. He did this after begging and praying of me to promise to say nothing for three days, which would enable the murderer to get out of England. I finally gave my word, and then hurried off to see my dear Arthur. I found him safe and well, but horrified by the murder he had witnessed."

"And you came away, leaving him there for three days more? Really, your Grace, I am surprised at you," said Holmes severely.

"They swore to do the boy no harm, and I could not risk James's being dragged into the murder, Mr. Holmes. After all, James is my son."

"I suppose you put up the money for Hayes to get away?" The duke nodded.

"And you were willing to expose your younger son to further danger to humor your guilty elder son?"

The proud lord of Holdernesse flushed crimson but said nothing.

"I will help you," Holmes finally said, "on one condition. Ring the bell for a servant, and let me give the order."

The duke pressed a bell. A footman entered.

"You will be glad to hear," said Holmes, "that your young master has been found. It is the duke's desire that the carriage go at once to the Fighting Cock Inn and bring Lord Saltire home." The rejoicing servant disappeared.

"Now," said Holmes, "I am not in an official position, so I can speak freely. Hayes is caught, and the gallows awaits him. You will have to take your chances on his talking to the police. They may be content to believe that he kidnapped the boy for ransom. Let us hope so. But I warn your Grace that Mr. Wilder should no longer be a member of your household."

"He is leaving me forever to seek his fortune in Australia."

"In that case, your Grace, since you have stated that the unhappiness between you and the duchess was caused by him, I suggest you try to make up with her."

"I have already written to her Grace this morning," said the duke.

"Good. Well, I think my friend and I may congratulate ourselves on a most happy conclusion to our little visit to the North. There is one more thing, your Grace, before we leave. This fellow Hayes had shod his horses with shoes which resembled the track of cows. Was it from Mr. Wilder that he learned the trick?"

The Duke looked surprised. Then he took us into a large room furnished as a museum. In a glass case in a corner of the room we saw the extraordinary horseshoes that were made to fit horses' hoofs, but which had underneath them the cloven foot of a cow, fashioned in iron. An inscription in the case stated that these shoes had been dug up in the old moat of Holdernesse Hall. They were supposed to have belonged to some robber barons of the Middle Ages, who used them to throw pursuers off their tracks.

Holmes opened the case, and moistening his finger, he passed it along a shoe. A thin film of recent mud was left upon his skin.

"Thank you," he said as he replaced the glass. "That is the second most interesting object I have seen in the North."

"And the first?" asked the Duke.

Holmes folded up the check and placed it carefully in his pocket book.

"I am a poor man," he said, as he patted it lovingly.

The Adventure of the Six Napoleons

One evening Inspector Lestrade was calling on Holmes and me. This was no unusual thing, as Lestrade was more of a friend than an official acquaintance. He often brought us news of what was going on at Scotland Yard. In return, Holmes would listen to the details of the latest case and offer advice, many times without actually engaging in the investigation himself.

On this particular evening, Lestrade had been puffing his cigar thoughtfully for some time without saying a word. Holmes looked keenly at him.

"Anything interesting on hand?" he asked.

"Oh, no, Mr. Holmes. Nothing very particular," answered Lestrade.

"Then tell me about it."

Lestrade laughed. "You are wonderful, Mr. Holmes! As a matter of fact, there *is* something. But it is a rather silly case, and seems to be more in Dr. Watson's line than ours."

"Disease?"

"Well, madness. A queer sort of madness, too. Here is a man who hates Napoleon Bonaparte so bitterly, he goes about breaking any statue of him he can find."

Holmes shrugged his shoulders and sank back in his chair. "That's hardly in my line," he said.

"No," answered Lestrade. "And it did not become our business, either, till the man committed burglary to get at some statues that were not his own. Then the police had to come into the picture."

"Burglary?" said Holmes, sitting up. "This is more interesting. Let me hear the details."

Lestrade refreshed his memory from his notebook, then told us what he knew.

"The first case was reported four days ago. It was at the shop of Morse Hudson, who has a picture and art shop in Kennington Road. The assistant had left the front of the shop for a moment when he heard a crash. Hurrying back, he found a plaster bust of Napoleon lying in fragments on the ground. He rushed out, and although the passers-by said that a man had just raced out of the shop, there was no sign of him then. The assistant put it down to some hoodlum or other and let it go at that. The bust was only worth a few shillings, anyhow.

"The second case, however, was more serious and very odd. It only happened last night.

"Within a few yards of this same art store, a Dr. Barnicot has his home and a consulting-office. He is an enthusiastic collector of Napoleon items, and had recently bought two busts of the little emperor from Morse Hudson. One of these he put in the hall of his house, and the other in his surgery in Lower Brixton Road.

"When Dr. Barnicot came downstairs on this very morning, it was to find that his house had been burglarized during the night, but that nothing had been taken except the plaster head of the French emperor. This had been carried out and dashed against the garden wall, where its splintered fragments were discovered."

Holmes rubbed his hands. "This is most unusual," said he. "Pray go on."

"I thought it would please you," said Lestrade. "Well, listen to this. When Dr. Barnicot got to his surgery in Lower Brixton Road this morning, he found that the window had been opened in the night, and the second bust taken from the mantelpiece and smashed all over the floor. Nothing else was touched, and, I might add, there are no clues as to the vandal who is doing this."

"Hm. Most unusual," repeated Holmes. "And were these two busts of Napoleon that Dr. Barnicot owned the exact copies of the one that was destroyed in the art store?"

"Oh, yes. They were made from the same mold."

"But there must be hundreds of pictures and statues of Napoleon in London. Why were only these three inexpensive ones destroyed?"

"I thought of that, too. But then, I figured that these were probably the only ones in that particular district."

"This is evidently the work of some fanatic who hates Napoleon for a personal reason," I suggested. "Perhaps his ancestors suffered through one of Napoleon's wars, and this man has brooded over it till he has lost his reason, and may even be a complete madman for all we know."

"Hardly, Watson," said Holmes. "I don't agree with your theory. Such a person would not go about his crazy work in such a neat way. Whoever did these acts of vandalism knew exactly what he was doing, and why. These are not the acts of a madman."

"Well, how do you explain it?"

"I don't attempt to do so. I only observe that there is a certain method in this strange person's actions. He was careful not to arouse the doctor's family in Kennington Road, carrying the statue out into the garden to some distance before smashing it. The whole thing seems unimportant.

Yet, I dare not call it unimportant when I remember the simple little things that started off some of my most famous cases. Do you remember, Watson, the case which began to unfold when I noticed how deep a bit of parsley had sunk into a piece of butter on a hot day? Let us know, Lestrade, if anything more develops."

Something did develop almost immediately, and it was far more tragic than either of us had expected. I was still dressing next morning when Holmes tapped at the door, then entered with a telegram in his hand, which read:

Come instantly, 131 Pitt Street, Kensington.

Lestrade

"I don't know what this is, but I suspect it is more about the man who breaks statues. There's coffee on the table, Watson. Drink it up. I have a cab at the door."

Holmes was already putting on his hat and coat.

In half an hour we reached Pitt Street, a quiet block of ordinary little dwellings. A curious crowd had already collected in front of No. 131. At sight of the people, Holmes whistled.

"Look, Watson, there's a messenger boy. The only thing that would make a London messenger loiter on his way would be murder, or attempted murder. Come on!"

We approached the front steps. "What's this?" commented Holmes. "The top steps have been washed and the lower ones left dry. Plenty of footsteps, though. Ah, there's Lestrade at the window. We shall soon know."

The police officer received us with an anxious face and then took us into the sitting room where a very untidy, elderly man, clad in a flannel dressing gown, was pacing up and down.

"This is Mr. Horace Harker of the Central Press Syndicate, gentlemen," said Lestrade, introducing us. "It's the Napoleon bust business again, Mr. Holmes. But it's very much more serious this time."

"What then?" said Holmes.

"It's murder this time, sir. Mr. Harker, will you tell these gentlemen just exactly what happened?"

The man in the dressing gown turned a long, gloomy face toward us.

"For the first time in my life, I have a newspaper scoop that I can't use myself. All I can do is to tell it over and over to a string of different people. Ah, well, Mr. Holmes, if you can help me, you are welcome to it."

We sat down and listened.

"It all seems to center around this bust of Napoleon that I picked up about four months ago. I got it cheap from Harding Brothers who have their place two doors from the High Street Station. I often work at night, and was doing so early this morning. I was sitting in my den at the back of the top of the house, about three o'clock, when I was sure I heard someone downstairs. I listened, but hearing nothing more, decided the noise came from outside.

"Then, suddenly, my blood was frozen by the most horrible yell—it was awful! I seized the poker, raced down here, found the window open and the plaster bust gone. Anyone could jump from the open window here to the front doorstep, so I rushed out and opened the door. As I stepped into the dark, I nearly fell over a dead man."

"Ah!" said Holmes.

"I ran back for a light, and there was the poor fellow, a great gash in his throat, and blood everywhere. He lay on his back, his knees drawn up, and his mouth hanging open." Harker shuddered. "I shall see him in my dreams. I had just time to blow on my police whistle and then I fainted, and came to in the hall with a policeman standing over me."

"Well, who was the murdered man?" asked Holmes.

"That's just what we don't know," said Lestrade. "There was nothing to show who he was."

"Well, well, what did he look like?"

"He is tall, about thirty, very powerful in build, and

somewhat sunburned. He is poorly dressed, and yet does not appear to be a laborer. A horn-handled knife was lying in a pool of blood beside him. We don't know if it was the murder weapon or not, or even if it belonged to him. No name was on his clothing. Nothing was in his pockets but an apple, some string, a cheap map of London, and a photograph. Here it is."

It was a small snapshot of an alert, sharp-featured man with thick eyebrows and a very strangely developed lower jaw. It reminded me of the muzzle of a baboon.

Holmes stared at the picture. "And the bust?" he said.

"Found in the front garden of an empty house in Campden House Road. Smashed, like the others. Shall we go and have a look at it?"

"In a moment," said Holmes. He was examining the carpet and the window. "The fellow either had long legs or was very active. It was hard to reach the window from the outside. Getting back was simple. Are you coming to see the remains of your bust, Mr. Harker?"

"I must write this up. A murder on my own doorstep does not happen every day, and I want to make the late papers with something new. Just my luck to lose the scoop!" He sighed deeply and bent over his work.

We left him busily writing and went to the spot where the bust had been found. It was quite near by and, for the first time, we saw for ourselves the evidence of this queer series of events. There lay the shattered face of the great emperor in splinters on the grass. From the way in which Holmes picked up some of them and examined them, I knew he had found a clue.

"Well?" said Lestrade.

"We have a long way to go yet," said Holmes. "But we do have some facts to begin with. Evidently the possession of this cheap bust was worth more to someone than a human life. Notice how careful he was to go to a safe distance to smash it, and notice, also, that we are standing in the garden of an empty house."

"He must have had to come where he would not be disturbed," said Lestrade.

"Yes, but why, then, did he not choose another empty house farther up the street which he must have passed before he came to this one? He took a terrible risk in carrying the bust this far."

"I give it up!" sighed Lestrade.

"Look!" Holmes pointed to the street lamp above our heads. "He came here so he could have light on what he was doing."

"That's right!" cried Lestrade. "Now that I come to think of it, Dr. Barnicot's bust was broken near his door light. What does that mean?"

"It means that we will remember this interesting little fact. It may come in handy later on. What are you going to do now, Lestrade?"

"We must first identify the dead man, I think. That ought to be easy. Then we can work from there. A study of the dead man's associates will probably tell us why he was in Pitt Street last night, also who met him and killed him on Harker's doorstep. Don't you think so?"

"Possibly. But I should not approach the case in that way."

"What would you do?"

"Oh, my way may be no better than yours. So you go your way, and I'll go mine. We can compare notes later."

"Very good," said Lestrade.

"Oh, by the way, you might stop at Harker's and tell him that I have quite made up my mind that a dangerous lunatic, with delusions about Napoleon, and bent on murder, was loose in his house last night. That might dress up his article a bit."

Lestrade stared.

"You don't really believe that, Mr. Holmes?"

Holmes smiled.

"Well, perhaps I don't. But you do as I suggest. The papers will pounce on it. Now, Watson, we have a long day's work ahead of us, and a hard one, too. Can you arrange to meet us at Baker Street tonight, Lestrade? About six o'clock, I should say. May I keep this photograph for the time being? And oh, yes, have your men ready. We may have to go on a little excursion tonight. That is, if my chain of reasoning proves correct. Now, good-bye, and good luck!"

Holmes and I then went to Harding Brothers' art store in High Street where Mr. Harker had bought the bust. A young assistant met us, and when Holmes learned that the owner would be out till the afternoon, his face darkened with disappointment.

"Well, well, Watson, we can't have it all our own way. Let us go on to Hudson's in Kennington Road, where the good doctor bought his two copies of the bust. I am anxious to find out if there is not something peculiar in these busts that makes them so attractive to a murderer."

The picture dealer in Kennington Road, a small, fat man

with a red face and a sharp temper, snorted angrily when we asked him about the bust that had been smashed in his own shop.

"In my opinion, sir," he said shortly, "you'll find it is a bunch of anarchists* who go about breaking such statues to show their hatred of kings and people of wealth."

We learned that the busts had been bought by him from the wholesale firm of Gelder & Co. in Church Street. Then Holmes showed him the photograph of the man with the monkey-like jaw. Did he know the man?

"No, I don't." Then he peered closer at it. "Yes, I do, though. I do! Why, it's Beppo. He was an Italian man who did piecework for me. He used to carve a bit, and gild, and make frames. He left me last week, and I've heard nothing since."

"Did you have anything against this man Beppo?" asked Holmes.

"No, nothing, nothing at all. He was gone two days before the bust was smashed."

As we left the shop, I could see that Holmes was pleased.

"Step number one," he said. "This Beppo is a common factor in both places. Now, let us go to the wholesaler in Church Street. We ought to get some good help there."

We found the sculpture works of Gelder & Co. deep in the waterside slums. Outside was a large yard full of white statuary. Inside in a large room about fifty workers were carving or molding. The manager, a big blond German, received us politely and answered clearly all Holmes's questions.

There had been hundreds of copies of this one bust, the original of which had been designed by a famous French sculptor. An interesting fact came to light when it was found that the three busts bought by the art dealer Hudson had been half of a batch of six. The other three had been bought by Harding Brothers.

---

*anarchists: people who seek to overthrow all forms of government.

The facts about the busts themselves were ordinary enough. They were cheaply made in the usual way. Two molds were taken, each of half the head. These were joined to make the complete head. The work was done by Italians in the room we were in.

But when Holmes showed the German the photograph of Beppo, the blond man's face flushed with anger and his blue eyes flashed.

"Ah, the rascal!" he cried. "Yes, indeed, I know him very well. He nearly got our establishment a bad name. He knifed a fellow Italian in the street, then came here to his work with the police on his heels. They took him away, and because the man got well, he got only one year. He is probably out now, but he dares not show his face here, I can tell you. We have his cousin with us, though, and I dare say he could tell you where the villain is."

"No, no," said Holmes. "Not a word to the cousin, I beg you. This matter is growing far too important to take any risks. I see by your records that the six Napoleon busts were sold on June 3 of last year. Could you give me the date on which this Beppo was arrested?"

"Well, I shall have to consult the pay list." The German turned to some books. "Ah, yes, here it is. He was last paid on May 20."

"Many thanks. And, not a word, please. Good day to you, sir."

We left and turned our faces westward once more. Toward the end of the afternoon, we snatched a hasty luncheon at a restaurant, and saw the late editions of the morning papers. They carried a full account of the story by Horace Harker, called, "Murder By a Madman." Holmes propped it up against the sugar basin and chuckled as he read it out to me.

"Listen to this, Watson. Harker ends his story by saying, 'Mr. Lestrade of the official force and Mr. Sherlock Holmes have come to the same conclusion. Both say this awful series of events must be the result of lunacy. No other explanation can be made.'

"And now," he said, as we finished, "if you are ready, we will stroll back to the firm of Harding Brothers and see what we can learn about their three busts."

Mr. Harding, the manager and owner, was in his office this time. He was a brisk, crisp little man, smartly dressed, and with a quick manner.

He was happy to answer our questions, and we soon found out what we wanted to know. In addition to the bust bought by Mr. Harker, the newspaperman, one other had been purchased by a Mr. Brown, who lived in Chiswick, just at the edge of the city, and the sixth one went to a Mr. Sandeford, of Reading, a town some miles away to the west.

Holmes seemed completely satisfied, and was in a hurry to be off, remarking that we should be late for our appointment with Lestrade. He thanked Mr. Harding, and we left at once for Baker Street. Sure enough, the detective was awaiting us, pacing up and down our rooms in a fever of impatience.

"Well?" he asked. "What luck, Mr. Holmes?"

"We have had a busy and quite fruitful day," my friend explained. "I now know where the busts came from and who has the lot in which we are interested."

"The busts!" cried Lestrade. "I never should have spent my time bothering with those. Well, well, you have your own way, Mr. Holmes, and it is not for me to say, but I fancy I have had a better day than you. I have identified the dead man."

"You don't say so!"

"Yes, and found a motive for the crime."

"Splendid!"

"Yes, I think so. I considered the fact that the dead man had a Catholic emblem around his neck, and that his complexion marked him as coming from Spain or Italy. My guess was Italy, and our inspector of the Italian quarter knew him instantly. His name is Pietro Venucci, and he comes from Naples. He is one of the greatest cut-throats in London."

"He belongs to a gang, I suppose?" said Holmes carelessly.

"That is so," agreed Lestrade. "Now, you see how the affair begins to clear up. The whole thing is a quarrel between two members of this outfit. The murdered man was obviously set to watch the other one. In order that he may not knife the wrong man, he carried a picture of his victim. He dogs his steps, watches him enter a house, waits outside for him, attacks him, and receives his own death wound. How's that, Mr. Sherlock Holmes?"

"Excellent, Lestrade, excellent!" cried Holmes. "But— the busts? What about them?"

"The busts! Your head is full of them, Mr. Holmes. The fellow was committing an act of petty larceny for reasons of his own, reasons that need not concern us. We are investigating murder, sir, not the destruction of a few cheap statues."

"What do you propose to do now?"

"It is very simple. We have the photo of the man we believe to be the murderer. All we have to do is to go down to the Italian quarter, find him, and arrest him. Will you come with us?"

"I think not. We have another even more important errand to do tonight. Our success depends upon one factor, over which we have no control, but the odds are two to one. What about your coming with us, and allowing me to present you with the murderer?"

"In the Italian quarter?"

"No, I propose to go to Chiswick. If you will come with us tonight, I promise to go with you tomorrow. Another slight delay cannot cause any harm. I suggest you have dinner with us, and then, let us all snatch a few hours of rest. I shall not leave till eleven, for I fancy we shall be up till morning. In the meantime, Watson, call an express messenger. I must send off a letter at once."

Lestrade agreed. I think he knew Holmes well enough to feel that in matters like this he could well afford to let his own theories stand while Holmes worked his out. He had great faith in Holmes, and was usually content to follow his judgment.

Holmes spent the evening in rummaging among the files of the old daily papers with which one of our storerooms was packed. When he came downstairs, there was a gleam in his eye, and I knew he was pleased with what he had found. He did not tell either of us what it was, but I felt sure that he expected the criminal to make an attempt upon one of the two remaining busts this very night. We were to go to Chiswick, and try to catch him in the act.

He had cleverly inserted a wrong clue, the theory that lunacy caused the crimes, in the evening papers, so as to throw the fellow off the track, and leave the field clear for him to make his next attempt. He suggested that I take my revolver, and he himself carried his favorite weapon, a hunting-crop with the head heavily loaded.

We took a four-wheeler at eleven, and drove to the other side of Hammersmith Bridge. Here the cabman was directed to wait, while we strolled down the road where Mr. Brown lived. On the gatepost of one of the houses, by the light of a streetlamp, we read his name, and the number of his house. The people within had all retired to rest, for the house was dark save for a dim light over the front door. At Holmes's direction, we crouched down in the shadow of a stout wooden fence that ran along the front of the yard.

"I'm afraid we shall have a long wait," he whispered. "And we dare not smoke. Thank goodness it is not raining. I think we shall not draw a blank, however, this time."

Our wait proved shorter than we thought, and came to an abrupt end. Without any warning at all, the garden gate swung open, and a dark figure glided noiselessly past us. The man slunk past the front of the house, and a moment later, we heard a faint creak as a window was pushed gently up. The noise ceased, and we then saw the flash of a dark lantern inside the room. The flash appeared in several other rooms as the burglar sought what he was after.

"Let us nab him as he comes out of the window," whispered Lestrade.

But before we could move, the man again appeared. He climbed out, and made for the street. As he came into the glimmering patch of light at the front door, we saw that he carried something white under his arm. He looked stealthily about him, then laid down his burden, and the next instant we heard a sharp rap, followed by a clatter and a rattle as he broke the bust.

He was so intent on what he was doing that he never heard our steps as we stole over the grass toward him. With the bound of a tiger Holmes was on his back, and an instant later Lestrade and I had him by the wrists and the handcuffs were on him. We turned him over and saw a hideous yellowish face, with rage and hate written all over it. It was Beppo, the man of the photograph.

But Holmes was no longer interested in the prisoner. Instead, he had squatted down on the doorstep and was ex-

amining the fragments of the broken bust. Carefully he held each splinter to the light. When he had just finished, the hall lights flew up, the door opened, and the owner of the house, a pleasant-faced fellow in shirt and trousers, presented himself.

"Mr. Josiah Brown, I presume?" said Holmes.

"Yes, sir. And you, sir, must be Mr. Sherlock Holmes. I got your message, all right, and I did exactly as you told me. I locked every door on the inside, and then sat tight. I am glad to see you have got the fellow. Will you come in and have some refreshment?"

But Lestrade was anxious to get his man locked up, so we thanked Mr. Brown, and resumed our seats in the cab, which had awaited us at Hammersmith Bridge. Our captive sat glaring at us with hatred, but saying nothing. Once, when my hand came too close to him, he snapped at it like a hungry wolf.

At the police station he was searched, but the only object worth noting was a long sheath knife, well stained with traces of recent blood.

"I still think my theory of the gang will explain this crime, Mr. Holmes, but all the same, I am greatly obliged to you for helping us to nab him. I don't quite understand how you did it."

"I am afraid this is hardly the time for explanations, inspector. There are one or two little details that are still to be worked out. Shall we meet at my rooms at about six o'clock tomorrow, when I hope to have all the pieces of the puzzle for you?"

When Lestrade came round to Baker Street the following evening, he had much more information concerning our prisoner. The only name by which he went was Beppo, and he was a familiar ne'er-do-well in the Italian quarter. He started life as a good sculptor, but took up evil ways, and had been twice in jail already. He stubbornly refused to tell why he went about London destroying busts of Napoleon, but the police had discovered that these busts might well have been made by his very hands. He did this work at the sculpture works of Gelder & Co. where he was employed under the blond German who had been so helpful to us.

Holmes listened to all this, but I could see that his mind was elsewhere. He seemed to be awaiting something, and this soon came, for I saw him start in his chair, and immediately afterward, the bell rang. An elderly red-faced man with grizzled whiskers was ushered in. He carried an old-fashioned carpetbag which he placed upon the table.

"Which gentleman is Mr. Sherlock Holmes?" he said, looking around.

My friend bowed and smiled. "You, sir, are Mr. Sandeford of Reading?"

"Yes, sir, and I fear I am a little late. The train connection was bad. You wrote to me about a bust that I have in my possession?"

"Exactly, and I presume you have brought it with you." Holmes pointed to the carpetbag. "As I said in my letter, I am prepared to pay you ten pounds for it."

"How did you know I owned such a thing?" asked Mr. Sandeford.

"Mr. Harding of Harding Brothers supplied me with that information."

"Then I suppose you also know I paid only fifteen shillings for the bust. I really do not see how I can accept such a large sum, Mr. Holmes. The object is not worth it."

"You are an honest man, Mr. Sandeford," smiled Holmes. "But that is the price, and I intend to stick to it."

Mr. Sandeford then opened the bag and took out the little Napoleon bust, the exact copy of the others we had seen. Holmes laid a ten-pound note on the table. He then handed our visitor a paper.

"You will kindly sign that paper, Mr. Sandeford, in the presence of these witnesses. It states that you assign to me this bust and resign any interest you ever had in it whatever. Thank you very much. There is your money, and I wish you good evening."

Mr. Sandeford shook his head, as if he thought Holmes

had lost his senses, but he pocketed the money, and taking up the empty carpetbag, withdrew. A moment later we heard the street door close behind him.

Sherlock Holmes now set about a curious task. He spread a clean white cloth over the table and set the bust in the center. Then he picked up his loaded hunting-crop and struck the bust a sharp blow on the top of the head. The figure broke into fragments, and Holmes immediately bent over the pieces. For a second he rummaged. Then he gave a loud shout. He held up one splinter in which a round, dark object was imbedded, for all the world like a plum in a pudding.

"Gentlemen," he cried, "let me introduce you to the famous black pearl of the Borgias."*

*Borgias: a famous Italian family of the Middle Ages.

Lestrade and I sat silent, lost in admiration of the supreme genius of this master detective. And then, we both clapped as if at a play. A slight flush of triumph crept into the pale cheeks of Holmes and he smiled self-consciously. Like any other human being, he loved applause.

"Yes, gentlemen," he said, "this is, by all odds, the most famous pearl in the world today. It disappeared from the bedroom of the Prince of Colonna at his hotel here in London, and now has turned up in the interior of this, the last of the six Napoleon busts manufactured by Gelder & Co.

"Remember, Lestrade, the sensation that the disappearance of this jewel caused. I myself worked on the case but was unable to turn up anything. Suspicion fell on the maid of the princess, who is undoubtedly the sister of this Pietro Venucci, since her name is Venucci, too. I looked up the date of the jewel's disappearance and found it was two days before Beppo was arrested for that crime of violence in the street, as you recall.

"And he had the pearl, stolen by this Lucretia Venucci, and given to him, perhaps, by her brother. They may have been in it together, or he may have stolen it from Venucci. That does not matter. He knew the police were hot on his trail because of the knifing in the street. He could not afford to be found with the pearl on him, so he hit on the very best place in the world in which to hide it.

"He imbedded it in the soft clay of one of the heads on which he was working, the moment before he was arrested. He spent a year in prison, for you remember, his victim recovered, and then when he got out, he began tracing the six busts all over London in the hope of finding the one in which he had hidden his stolen treasure."

"But where does Pietro Venucci come into this?" I asked.

"Pietro no doubt held Beppo responsible for the loss of the pearl, and searched London for him. He had just caught up with him and surprised him leaving Harker's when Beppo stabbed him to death."

"But I do not understand why he had to carry a photograph of his confederate," I insisted.

"That was so he could show it to people and ask if they had seen Beppo."

"I see," I said, embarrassed that I had not thought of this myself.

"Beppo had to hurry now. It would only be a little while before the police would start on his trail, and he had not yet found the pearl. The search narrowed down to two busts, one on the edge of London, the other one farther away. I reasoned he would go for the London one first. I warned Mr. Brown to expect trouble, and after the happy results of our little trip to Chiswick, I knew the pearl had to be in the one remaining bust, the one owned by Mr. Sandeford of Reading."

Holmes paused. "I bought it," he said, "and there the pearl lies."

"Well," said Lestrade, "I've seen you handle many a case, Mr. Holmes, but I have never seen a more workmanlike job than this. We're not jealous of you down at Scotland Yard! No, sir, we're proud to be associated with you. Come down tomorrow, and let all the rest of us shake your hand."

"Thank you," said Holmes, "thank you."

He turned away but not before I was surprised by an unusual expression on his cold, pale face. It was slightly quivering with emotion, more so than I had ever seen it. It was plain to be seen that the appreciation expressed by his friend Lestrade had touched him deeply.

A moment more, and he was the same cold and practical Holmes.

"Put the pearl in the safe, Watson, and get out those papers we were working on in that other robbery case. Good-bye, Lestrade. If any little problem comes your way, I shall be happy, if I can, to give you a hint or two as to its solution."

Other Sherlock Holmes Adventures

A Study in Scarlet
This is a novelette in which Holmes solves his first case, a murder among the Mormons of Utah.

The Hound of the Baskervilles
This, perhaps the most terrifying of all the adventures, takes place on the Devon moors. Holmes solves the secret of the terrible man-killing hound of the Baskerville family.

The Missing Three-Quarter
This is an account of some strange adventures that befall a college football player.

The Five Orange Pips
A man receives a letter in which there are five dried-up orange pips, or pits. The murder chase leads to the United States.

The Musgrave Ritual
A secret trap door and a giant checkerboard are two of the weird objects in this story of an Old English family.

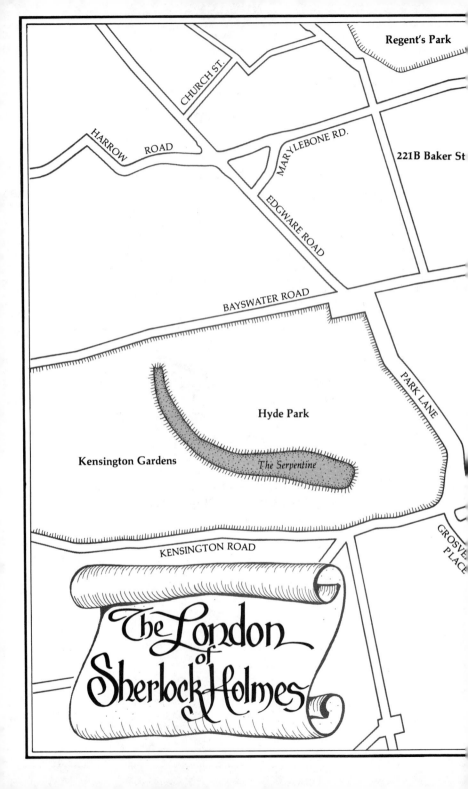

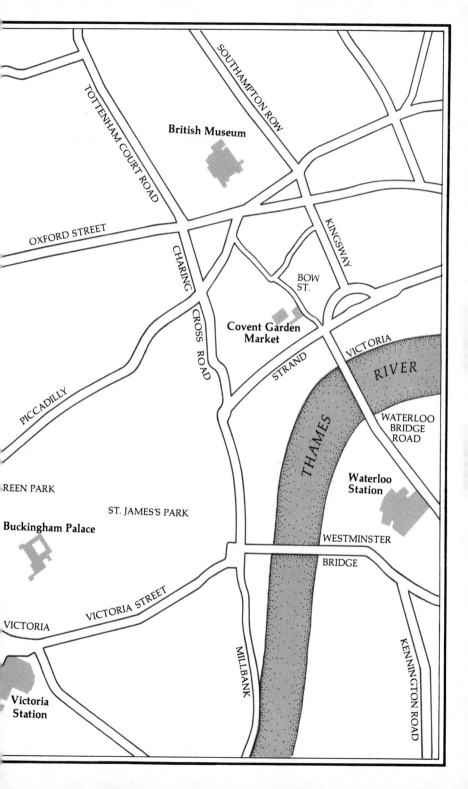

Reviewing Your Reading

A Word from Dr. Watson

Finding the Main Idea
1. Dr. Watson wrote this letter in order to
   (A) describe the city of London (B) discuss his army career (C) introduce Sherlock Holmes (D) tell about Mycroft Holmes

Remembering Detail
2. Holmes's friend Lestrade was a member of the
   (A) police force (B) largest gang in London (C) Holmes family (D) British army in Afghanistan
3. The long-suffering landlady at Baker Street was named
   (A) Mrs. Mycroft (B) Mrs. Kensington (C) Mrs. Stamford (D) Mrs. Hudson
4. Watson began his career as an army doctor in
   (A) London (B) India (C) Scotland (D) Russia

Drawing Conclusions
5. Holmes was a master detective because he drew his conclusions based on
   (A) lucky guesses (B) careful observations (C) long research (D) newspaper stories

Using Your Reason
6. One reason why Sherlock Holmes became so famous was because
   (A) his brother was very lazy (B) Watson wrote stories of their adventures (C) he often worked in Russia and Holland (D) he was a master of disguises

7. You can tell that Watson was more interested in being a detective than a doctor by the way he
(A) took holidays to travel with Holmes (B) used his service revolver (C) described his medical practice (D) often worked on his own cases

Identifying the Mood

8. Holmes's attitude toward Watson's careful accounts of their cases was one of
(A) disgust (B) envy (C) amusement (D) pride

Thinking It Over

1. Do you think Watson was a good doctor? Why or why not?
2. Holmes said that for a doctor, Watson was very unscientific when he wrote up the stories of their adventures. What do you think Holmes meant by this? Why do you think Watson was unscientific in writing about his friend?

The Adventure
of the Speckled Band

Finding the Main Idea
1. This story is mostly about
   (A) a gypsy band (B) a young woman's strange death
   (C) the theft of a necklace (D) a railroad accident

Remembering Detail
2. What did Julia Stoner hear several nights before she died?
   (A) Animal cries (B) A song (C) A whistle (D) Laughter
3. Julia was killed in
   (A) her bedroom (B) the yard (C) the village (D) her aunt's house
4. What was suspicious about Julia's bedroom?
   (A) It had strange fingerprints. (B) It had no fireplace.
   (C) The door had no lock. (D) The bed was nailed to the floor.
5. Julia Stoner was killed by a
   (A) snake (B) baboon (C) cheetah (D) spider
6. Holmes trapped Dr. Roylott by
   (A) following him to London (B) waiting for his next attack (C) opening his safe (D) sending him a fake message
7. How did Dr. Roylott die?
   (A) Holmes shot him. (B) The cheetah attacked him.
   (C) His snake bit him. (D) A gypsy killed him.

Drawing Conclusions
8. Dr. Roylott didn't want his stepdaughters to get married because he
   (A) didn't like their boyfriends (B) didn't want to live alone (C) was not told of their engagements (D) would have to give them large sums of money

9. Helen herself was in danger when she finally went to Holmes because she
   (A) was going to be married (B) knew what killed Julia
   (C) threatened her stepfather (D) moved out of the house

10. What clues made Holmes think that Dr. Roylott had a snake?
    (A) Hissing noises in the safe (B) Marks in the soil
    (C) A dish of milk and small dog leash (D) Dead mice on the bed

Using Your Reason

11. Holmes says that he is probably responsible for the death of the doctor, "but I cannot say that it is likely to weigh very heavily upon my conscience." He would have meant the same think if he had said that he
    (A) feels very guilty (B) is not going to worry about it
    (C) should have tried to stop it (D) planned it that way

12. If Julia struck a match before she died, you can figure out that she might have seen
    (A) a "speckled band" (B) Dr. Roylott (C) a ghost
    (D) the gypsies

13. When Helen told Holmes that she heard a whistle while staying in her sister's room, it seemed likely that
    (A) she had been dreaming (B) the gypsy band had been breaking in (C) the snake had been in the bedroom
    (D) she had been lying

Thinking It Over

1. Explain Holmes's statement that doctors make "the greatest criminals." Why do you think he came to that conclusion? Do you agree or disagree?

2. What was Dr. Roylott's biggest mistake as a murderer? Do you think he was careless? Why or why not?

3. Do you think the Stoner sisters were foolish to live with their stepfather for so long? Was there anything else they could have done? Explain your answers.

The Adventure of the
Man With the Twisted Lip

Finding the Main Idea

1. This story is mostly concerned with
(A) an opium den (B) a man's disappearance (C) a beggar's murder (D) an opium addict

Remembering Detail

2. Watson went into the opium den in order to
(A) smoke opium (B) look for Sherlock Holmes (C) look for a friend (D) investigate a murder

3. Whom did Watson unexpectedly meet?
(A) Isa Whitney (B) The police (C) Neville St. Clair (D) Sherlock Holmes

4. Mrs. St. Clair called the police when she
(A) found money hidden in the house (B) could not find her husband (C) saw her husband in a room over an opium den (D) was told to do so by Holmes

5. What did Neville St. Clair do in the room over the opium den?
(A) Change into a beggar's costume (B) Smoke opium (C) Hide from the police (D) Plan robberies

6. St. Clair's coat pockets were filled with pennies in order to
(A) frame Boone for a robbery (B) hide the money (C) sink the coat in the river (D) make Neville look like a beggar

7. Mrs. St. Clair knew that her husband was alive five days after he disappeared because she
(A) received a letter from him (B) saw him on the train (C) dreamt about him (D) knew he was in jail

Drawing Conclusions

8. In the beginning of the story, Holmes was in the opium den because he wanted to
   (A) smoke opium (B) investigate the den (C) spy on the owner (D) get information
9. The police concluded that St. Clair had been murdered because they found
   (A) a great deal of blood in the room (B) signs of struggle (C) his coat in the river (D) a murder weapon
10. Neville St. Clair became a beggar because he was
    (A) crippled from birth (B) forced into it (C) out of a job (D) able to earn a lot of money

Using Your Reason

11. You can figure out that the beggar refused to wash because he wanted to
    (A) annoy the police (B) take a nap (C) stay dirty (D) keep his make-up on
12. You can probably figure out that the person who would be most upset about Neville's adventure is
    (A) Mrs. St. Clair (B) Sherlock Holmes (C) the den owner (D) Inspector Bradstreet
13. St. Clair was a successful beggar because
    (A) he was clever and entertaining (B) Londoners were kind-hearted (C) he was badly crippled (D) he was also a pickpocket

Identifying the Mood

14. When Neville St. Clair saw his wife through the window, he cried out in
    (A) terror (B) surprise (C) anger (D) delight
15. When Holmes had an unsolved problem, he could go for days without
    (A) laughing (B) smoking (C) moving (D) sleeping

Thinking It Over

1. Go back to the story and find all of the facts you can about the opium den. What conclusions can you draw about the London of Sherlock Holmes? Do you think opium dens can operate legally in London today? Why or why not?

2. St. Clair would rather have stayed in jail than admit that he was a beggar. Do you think his behavior was extreme? What were his reasons?

3. Why do you think that Mrs. St. Clair was not curious about her husband's job? Would you have been curious? Why or why not?

The Adventure
of the Blue Carbuncle

Finding the Main Idea

1. This story is mostly concerned with the mystery of who (A) robbed an elderly man (B) raised a certain goose (C) murdered a farmer (D) stole a gem

2. Another title for this story might be (A) "The Goose That Laid the Golden Egg" (B) "A Christmas Goose Recipe" (C) "Identical Geese" (D) "The Stolen Goose"

Remembering Detail

3. In the beginning of the story, Holmes studied a hat that belonged to (A) Peterson (B) a man who was robbed (C) a suspected thief (D) Watson

4. Henry Baker got his Christmas goose directly from (A) Covent Garden Market (B) the landlord of his club (C) Mrs. Oakshott (D) Hotel Cosmopolitan

5. What did Mrs. Peterson find in the crop of the goose? (A) A diamond (B) A blue stone (C) A ring (D) A necklace

Drawing Conclusions

6. You can figure out that Henry Baker didn't know what was inside his goose because he (A) accepted a substitute goose (B) dropped the goose when he was attacked (C) received the goose as a present (D) advertised for the goose

7. When Holmes got into an argument with Mr. Breckenridge about the goose, he really wanted to (A) win some money (B) see how it was raised (C) find out who raised it (D) find out who bought it

Using Your Reason

8. In the beginning of the story, Watson couldn't tell anything about the hat because he could not
    (A) see small details (B) figure out what details meant
    (C) try hard enough (D) smell the lime cream

9. Holmes reasoned that the owner of the hat had lost his money because the hat was
    (A) cheap (B) expensive but old (C) dirty and torn
    (D) large

10. The police blamed the plumber for the robbery of the Blue Carbuncle because he
    (A) was seen by several witnesses (B) had a police record (C) had the jewel case (D) was in debt

11. Holmes knew that Ryder was involved with the theft because Ryder
    (A) tried to break into Holmes's rooms (B) tried to kill Holmes (C) advertised for the missing hat (D) tried to find out who bought the goose

12. Ryder had forced the carbuncle down the goose's throat because he wanted to
    (A) play a practical joke (B) frame his sister for the theft (C) hide it from the police (D) pass it on to his friend

13. Which of the following is the most illogical part of the story?
    (A) That the owner of the hat was smart because he had a large head (B) That Mr. Baker knew nothing about the Blue Carbuncle (C) That the police would suspect the man with a prison record (D) That Holmes could make Breckinridge talk by means of making a bet

14. From the way Holmes could handle different types of people, you can tell that he
    (A) understood people very well (B) couldn't understand people (C) frightened people (D) didn't like people

15. Holmes's career as a detective is successful largely because he is a talented
(A) doctor (B) actor (C) farmer (D) businessman

Reading for Deeper Meaning
16. What did Holmes consider the worst part of Ryder's crime?
(A) Framing an innocent man (B) Stealing the gem
(C) Lying about it (D) Disappointing his parents

Thinking It Over
1. Why did Holmes let Ryder go? Would you have done the same thing?
2. Holmes told Watson that by letting Ryder go, he was perhaps committing a felony. Do you think that Holmes had the same responsibility to the law that a law officer would have? Explain your answer.
3. What was Holmes's attitude toward jewels and great wealth? Use examples from the story to support your answer.

The Adventure
of the Final Problem

Finding the Main Idea

1. This story is concerned with
   (A) a Swiss master criminal (B) the death of Holmes
   (C) Holmes's vacation (D) a gang of thieves

Remembering Detail

2. According to Holmes, what was unusual about Professor Moriarty?
   (A) No one had heard of him. (B) He was a mathematician. (C) He was a genius. (D) He was after Holmes.
3. How was Moriarty involved in crime?
   (A) He was a burglar. (B) He organized crimes. (C) He was the head of a small gang. (D) He designed weapons.
4. Why was Holmes still in danger after the arrest of Moriarty's gang?
   (A) Moriarty's brother wanted revenge. (B) Moriarty's right-hand man escaped. (C) Moriarty escaped. (D) A new criminal organization took over London.
5. How did Holmes and Moriarty apparently die?
   (A) In a duel (B) By falling over a cliff (C) In an avalanche (D) By taking poison

Drawing Conclusions

6. Holmes probably told Watson not to take the first or second hansom cab that came along because
   (A) they had plenty of time (B) the cabs might have been sent by Moriarty (C) Holmes wanted to confuse Moriarty (D) Holmes didn't know where he wanted to go
7. Moriarty visited Holmes in his rooms in order to
   (A) kill him (B) threaten him (C) bargain with him (D) spy on him

8. Holmes and Watson left the country so that
(A) Holmes would be safe until Moriarty's arrest
(B) they could go on another case (C) Watson could go
on vacation (D) they could follow Moriarty
9. Watson was really called back to the hotel because
(A) a guest needed him   (B) Moriarty wanted to
get Holmes alone   (C) Watson had to pay the bill
(D) Holmes needed help

Using Your Reason

10. You can figure out that the incidents with the van and
the brick were
(A) murderous attacks   (B) warnings   (C) accidents
(D) practical jokes
11. Watson described Lake Daubensee as "melancholy."
He would have meant the same thing if he had said
that the lake was
(A) delightful (B) very quiet (C) gloomy (D) very busy

Identifying the Mood

12. When Holmes visited Watson in the consulting room, he
was afraid of being
(A) robbed (B) killed (C) kidnapped (D) overheard
13. What did Holmes feel towards Moriarty?
(A) Fear and envy   (B) Horror mixed with admiration
(C) Profound respect (D) Contempt
14. Which word best describes the way Holmes faced death?
(A) Cooly (B) Cowardly (C) Nervously (D) Regretfully

Thinking It Over

1. What did Holmes think was his responsibility to society?
Support your answer with evidence from this story.
2. When Arthur Conan Doyle became tired of writing about
Sherlock Holmes, he decided to have Holmes die. Think
about the way Holmes acted in the other stories. Do you

think his behavior in this story is reasonable? How could
he have protected himself better?
3. How was Professor Moriarty especially suited to a life of
crime?

The Return of Sherlock Holmes

Finding the Main Idea

1. This story is mostly about how
   (A) Holmes posed as a Norwegian explorer (B) Watson investigated crime on his own (C) Holmes survived his battle with Moriarty (D) Holmes solved Ronald Adair's murder

2. Another title for this story might be
   (A) "Dr. Watson Turns Detective" (B) "The Park Lane Mystery" (C) "The Real Solution to the Final Problem" (D) My Life as a Norwegian Explorer"

Remembering Detail

3. Watson didn't recognize Holmes at first because Holmes was
   (A) much older   (B) in a disguise   (C) very sickly (D) dirty and ragged

4. What really happened at Reichenbach Falls?
   (A) Neither Holmes nor Moriarty fell over the cliff. (B) Holmes survived the fall. (C) Holmes shot Moriarty. (D) Only Moriarty fell over the cliff.

5. During the three years since his disappearance, Holmes
   (A) pursued his enemies in England   (B) traveled and studied   (C) investigated crimes in Europe   (D) wrote mystery stories

6. The only person Holmes had told of his escape from death was
   (A) his brother (B) Inspector Lestrade (C) Mrs. Hudson (D) Ronald Adair

7. Holmes had to tell someone that he was alive because he was in need of
(A) food (B) a place to hide from his enemies (C) money (D) help in getting out of the country
8. This story took place in the spring of
(A) 1849· (B) 1894 (C) 1914 (D) 1918

Drawing Conclusions
9. Holmes decided to come back to England because he
(A) was working for the government (B) became interested in the Adair murder (C) ran out of money (D) was tired of traveling
10. Holmes walked ten miles over the mountains after Moriarty died because he
(A) lost his way (B) wanted to leave before the police came (C) wanted to hide from Watson (D) knew Moriarty's agent had seen the struggle
11. Holmes realized that someone knew he was still alive when he
(A) came face to face with Mycroft in London (B) saw a head above him at the falls (C) discovered that he was being followed in Egypt (D) was nearly killed in a laboratory in the south of France

Using Your Reason
12. Watson's reason for visiting the scene of Adair's murder was that he was
(A) the family doctor (B) looking for Holmes (C) interested in crime (D) invited by the police
13. Holmes pretended to be dead for three years because
(A) he wanted to live a double life (B) he would have been arrested for Moriarty's death (C) three dangerous criminals had sworn to kill him (D) he became a government spy
14. Holmes hadn't told Watson that he was alive because he thought Watson would give him away by

(A) telling the police (B) trying to contact him (C) telling Moriarty's gang (D) writing a story

Identifying the Mood
15. What was Watson's immediate reaction when he first saw Holmes?

    (A) Shock (B) Delight (C) Terror (D) Disappointment

Thinking It Over
1. Do you think Holmes was right to keep his existence a secret for three years? Why or why not?
2. What do Holmes's activities during those three years tell you about Holmes's talents?
3. Holmes thought he was in danger for three years. What does this tell you about the kind of enemies he had? Why would they be so determined to destroy Holmes?
4. Do you think Watson might have felt mixed emotions when he saw Holmes alive again after three years? Do you think he might have been angry at Holmes for not contacting him during that time? Explain your answer.

The Adventure
of the Empty House

Finding the Main Idea

1. The main idea of this story is that Holmes
   (A) figures out a puzzling crime (B) returns to Baker Street (C) traps Adair's killer (D) is shot by Colonel Moran

Remembering Detail

2. Where was the house that Holmes and Watson waited in?
   (A) In a London slum (B) On the riverfront (C) Opposite Holmes's rooms in Baker Street (D) Behind Watson's home

3. What did Watson see in Holmes's window?
   (A) An intruder (B) A rifle (C) A wax bust of Holmes (D) A lantern

4. When Colonel Moran entered the empty house, he
   (A) shot Holmes (B) shot the figure in the window (C) watched Baker Street (D) signaled to his men

5. Holmes had expected that Colonel Moran would
   (A) not fall for the trap (B) miss the target (C) use a hired killer (D) shoot from the street

6. What did Lestrade charge Moran with?
   (A) Breaking and entering (B) The attempted murder of Sherlock Holmes (C) The murder of Ronald Adair (D) Cheating at cards

Drawing Conclusions

7. The figure in the window was turned every fifteen minutes so that it would
   (A) seem more like a real person (B) scare the spies on the street (C) attract the spies' attention (D) keep out of rifle range

Using Your Reason

8. Moriarty's men were watching Baker Street day and night because they
   (A) knew Holmes was alive and would return to it
   (B) wanted to break in and steal the evidence
   (C) wanted to find Mycroft   (D) wanted to kill Holmes's client

9. Colonel Moran killed Adair because Adair
   (A) cheated him at cards   (B) caught Moran cheating at cards   (C) blackmailed him   (D) turned him over to the police

10. Moran tried to kill Holmes because he
    (A) thought Holmes was connected with the murder investigation   (B) wanted to avenge Moriarty's death
    (C) wanted some secret papers that belonged to Holmes
    (D) wanted to start a new criminal organization

11. Holmes felt that as a criminal, Moran was
    (A) more dangerous than Moriarty   (B) only second to Moriarty   (C) cowardly but vicious   (D) merely the tool of some bigger criminals

Identifying the Mood

12. In this story, Holmes is described as being
    (A) cool   (B) relaxed   (C) confident and carefree   (D) excited and tense

Reading for Deeper Meaning

13. Holmes would probably agree that great talents will
    (A) prevent people from becoming criminals   (B) never be found in criminals   (C) always make people into criminals   (D) make some people into great criminals

Thinking It Over

1. Holmes seemed surprised that his trick really fooled Colonel Moran. Are you surprised too? Do you think it was a clever trick? Why or why not?

2. In what ways was Mrs. Hudson an unusual landlady?
3. What are some of the ways in which Watson helps Holmes on his adventures? Use examples from this story.
4. What are some of the ways in which Holmes showed his pride in this story?

The Adventure
of the Priory School

Finding the Main Idea

1. This story is mostly concerned with
   (A) a German teacher's murder (B) the disappearance of
   Lord Saltire (C) the duke's treatment of employees
   (D) the duke's separation from his wife

Remembering Detail

2. How did Lord Saltire leave the school?
   (A) He climbed out of his window. (B) Two men kidnapped him. (C) He pretended to visit his father. (D) He
   ran away during a field trip.

3. Who else was missing?
   (A) Dr. Huxtable (B) The boy's mother (C) The duke
   (D) Heidegger, the German teacher

4. In the swamp near the school, Holmes found the tracks
   of
   (A) horses (B) bicycles (C) a cart (D) a car

5. The German teacher had been killed by a
   (A) fall (B) heavy blow on the head (C) bullet wound
   in the chest (D) bull

6. Lord Saltire was being held in
   (A) the Fighting Cock Inn (B) the swamp (C) Holdernesse Hall (D) the south of France

Drawing Conclusions

7. Holmes thought he could find tracks in the swamp because
   (A) it hadn't rained since the kidnapping (B) the boy
   was hiding there (C) the police hadn't looked there
   (D) the moist ground would take good impressions

8. Holmes probably pretended to sprain his ankle near the
   inn to see if the landlord had

(A) a bicycle (B) bandages (C) visitors (D) a gun

9. Hayes was able to fool Holmes at first by
    (A) changing the tires of his bicycle (B) retracing his
    steps to the school (C) using horseshoes that looked
    like cow's feet (D) traveling through water to hide
    his tracks

10. James Wilder kidnapped the boy in order to
     (A) force the duke to change his will (B) kill the boy
     (C) blackmail the duchess (D) win the reward for find-
     ing the boy

Using Your Reason

11. Holmes knew that Dr. Huxtable had waited three days
     to see him because of the
     (A) railroad ticket (B) growth of beard on Huxtable's
     chin (C) newspaper article (D) dark circles around
     Huxtable's eyes

12. Heidegger had gone into the swamp because he had
     (A) lost his way (B) kidnapped the boy (C) tried to
     ambush the boy (D) followed the boy

13. Holmes felt that James Wilder was responsible for the
     death of Heidegger because Wilder
     (A) accidentally struck the man (B) made the landlord
     kill the man (C) planned the kidnapping (D) murdered
     the man

Reading for Deeper Meaning

14. Holmes disapproved of the duke mostly for
     (A) loving his eldest son (B) endangering the life of his
     younger son (C) sending the boy to boarding school
     (D) helping the landlord escape

Thinking It Over

1. How do you think Holmes felt toward nobles? Why do
    you think Holmes was so delighted to receive the check

from the duke? Was he just greedy? Explain your answers.

2. Huxtable told Holmes and Watson that the duke offered a reward of six thousand pounds for the return of his son. When Holmes accused the duke, the duke said "I believe the amount I owe you is twelve thousand pounds." Do you think the duke made a mistake? Why did he double the amount of the reward?

3. Holmes stood on Watson's back to see who came to visit James Wilder at the Fighting Cock Inn, but he did not tell Watson who he saw. When did you realize that Holmes had seen the duke? Why do you think the author did not identify the duke as Wilder's visitor until later?

The Adventure
of the Six Napoleons

Finding the Main Idea

1. This story is mostly concerned with why someone
   (A) smashed busts of Napoleon (B) hated Napoleon
   (C) bought a Napoleon statue (D) murdered a sculptor

Remembering Detail

2. The odd thing about the vandal was that he or she
   (A) always left money for the stolen bust (B) broke·
   only copies of a particular Napoleon statue (C) always
   cleaned up afterward (D) destroyed paintings as well as
   statues

3. What important clue did the murdered man have to
   the identity of the vandal?
   (A) A piece of clothing (B) Strands of hair (C) His
   name and address (D) A photograph

4. Who was Beppo?
   (A) The murdered man (B) The art dealer (C) The man
   in the photograph (D) The owner of the Napoleon
   figures

5. What linked Beppo to the statues?
   (A) He had worked where the statues were made.
   (B) He hated Napoleon. (C) The picture dealer had
   fired him for theft. (D) He collected Napoleon statues.

Drawing Conclusions

6. The vandal always smashed the statues near a light because he wanted to look for
   (A) something in the statue (B) the police (C) his ac-
   complice (D) the man who was following him

7. Lestrade's biggest mistake on this case was that he
   (A) didn't investigate the murder (B) didn't link the

murder with the statue breaking (C) couldn't identify the victim (D) didn't go to the Italian quarter in London

Using Your Reason

8. Holmes first became interested in the smashing of the statues because it was
(A) methodical (B) pointless (C) vicious (D) insane
9. Holmes misled the newspapers about the murder because he
(A) didn't know the truth (B) didn't want to scare the murderer away (C) wanted the police to look foolish (D) wanted the reporter to get a good story
10. How did Holmes predict that Beppo would strike at Mr. Brown's house?
(A) Beppo had once worked for Mr. Brown. (B) Beppo had followed Mr. Brown. (C) Mr. Brown had the last Napoleon bust. (D) Mr. Brown's home was closer than Mr. Sandeford's.
11. Beppo's reason for smashing the busts was that he wanted to
(A) find a black pearl (B) distract the police (C) get even with the art dealer (D) scare political enemies
12. Beppo killed Venucci because Venucci
(A) had the black pearl (B) held Beppo responsible for the loss of the pearl (C) turned Beppo in to the police (D) knew where the pearl was

Identifying the Mood

13. When Lestrade praised him, Holmes was
(A) moved (B) embarrassed (C) contemptuous (D) annoyed

Thinking It Over

1. Describe Holmes's relationship with Lestrade and the police force. Use examples from this story to support your answer.

2. What was Holmes's attitude toward the trivial things he came across on a case? Do you think detectives today have the same attitude? Use examples from your reading, TV, or movies to support your answer.

3. Why was Holmes's method of investigating the murder and linking it to the smashing of the statues, better than Inspector Lestrade's method?

4. At times, Watson seems to describe Holmes as a man with little or no human emotions. At other times, however, Holmes seems to show signs of being a very real person. Which side of Holmes does Watson seem to stress in this story? Give examples from the story to support your answer.